———— ★ ————

"I'M NEXT OF KIN."

Lennox Kemp eyed him speculatively. More than kin and less than kind.... The will—or lack of one—that would be the trend of Lindsay's thoughts.

"There is a husband," he observed mildly as he went to the door.

"Murdering bastard..." muttered Lindsay, but he got to his feet and held out a hand to Kemp. "We're in this thing together, you and I. It's for us to see that he doesn't get away with it."

But Kemp wasn't certain on either proposition. He preferred to take his own path, as he had always done, finding it the better way to discover truth and ultimately see justice done.

———— ★ ————

"Solidly entertaining story that effectively evokes the look, climate and speech of Scotland."
—*Kirkus Reviews*

THE SPLIT SECOND

M.R.D. MEEK

WORLDWIDE®

TORONTO · NEW YORK · LONDON · PARIS
AMSTERDAM · STOCKHOLM · HAMBURG
ATHENS · MILAN · TOKYO · SYDNEY

For my brother,
JIMMY GILLORAN—
because of Bute

THE SPLIT SECOND

A Worldwide Mystery/November 1989

This edition is reprinted by arrangement with Charles Scribner's Sons, a division of Macmillan, Inc.

ISBN 0-373-26035-0

PART ONE

ONE

Even in the Waters of the Firth there be Sharks....

THEY LAY CALM and sparkling, the waters of the Firth in the cold October sunshine, calm, sparkling and very boring. Fiona turned from the rail of the Largs Esplanade and sighed. It was ten o'clock on a Sunday morning, and ennui had set in early. All the good people were dressing for church, psalms and paraphrases already in the back of their minds, hats and gloves to the forefront, children roundly chided, husbands' shoulders smartly brushed, lean breakfasts adequately digested. The long process of the Sabbath had begun.

Fiona looked back at the town. Most of it was still asleep despite lazy smoke ascending from wakened chimneys. Old red sandstone cliff and beach, the spires of churches, sky-pointing fingers of righteousness among the new excrescences of long white hotels, dance halls now autumnally deserted but flaunting their peeling sweetie-pink paint careless of appearance, and the ice-cream parlours—Fiona wondered if they were still so described, her knowledge of them hopelessly old-fashioned—lending casual modernity to the Presbyterian past. She sighed again. I've chosen the wrong place, she thought; I should have gone straight to the Bahamas. But that was a flight of fancy too sickening to contemplate. She turned again and looked across to Rothesay still abed in the fold of its island. I should have gone to Rothesay; Mother never would. Said it was common, a vulgar place. It would have been a tiny act of bravado to have gone there, Mother would not have expected it. Fiona had vowed to do things gradually, treat her new-found freedom carefully, take one step at a time, proceed at a measured pace. Just as when she had raised herself from her mother's deathbed she had wanted to fling her arms in the air and rejoice, then had sobered instantly not only because it would have seemed an outlandish gesture to old Dr. Farebrother, waiting and ready with conventional commiseration, but because her whole nature had been so circumscribed that such tumultuous feeling would have been as quickly reined in to accord with the decorum expected of her. So, having taken this small step, this first holiday on her own, she had gone no further than fifty miles from her home, and stayed safe on familiar territory.

It had seemed adventure enough to have left immediately after the properly conducted funeral rites. Her mother was dead. She would not be especially mourned, either by Fiona herself or by the decreasing number of relatives and friends whose affection, like hers, had been worn threadbare over the years by the incessant demands and whims of a well-to-do invalid upon whom even age had had no softening impact; selfish, domineering and petulant Anna Davison-Maclean had been in her girlhood and had remained so throughout her life, which had now satisfactorily closed. Fiona, the daughter and only child, having given not her best years—since she hoped these were still to come with the enjoyment of her mother's estate and fortune—but surely her whole being to the service of such a creature, now felt the future opening up before her in a splendid dazzle of liberty.

All that in fact opened out before her at this moment, however, was the static grace of a Scottish watering-place at the back-end of the season.

She had booked into what was in summer a busy luxury hotel bustling with tourists anxious to get their full mileage out of the swimming pools, saunas and ornamental gardens but now putting a brave face on a trickle of old-age pensioners and a few reps scanning their Christmas order books who felt their expense sheets could stand the lowered terms. One of these gentlemen of the road had spoken to Fiona at breakfast, giving her a respectful good morning and remarking on the weather.

Turning now from the view of some of the most seductive scenery in the western hemisphere, and knowing it to be so from long indoctrination in the picturesque, Fiona was unimpressed. This wholesome vista of blue sea, and low green islands with the distant hazy mountains of Arran uplifting their arrogant peaks as if to disclaim alike the attrition of weather and the admiration of visitors, held no interest for her. Mrs. Davison-Maclean had valued scenery as she had the jewellery in her boxes, the clothes in her wardrobes, the stocks and shares in her bank; something of that same attitude had brushed off on Fiona. She had never lacked the opportunity to contemplate the beauties of nature. As a child she had been bored by endless journeys to see waterfalls, and lochs, pine forests and long silver beaches; she had never been allowed to partake of them, to grasp them as things she could play with. Only once when her father had let her take the tiller of his yacht had she known pure happiness—but that was a long time ago.

She could give no name to her present dissatisfaction—too soon to call it discontent—it was only that she felt there must be more to life than this.

In short, Fiona Davison-Maclean was ripe for exploitation.

That she was to be split open in the process was, mercifully, screened from her as she walked, neat in her tweed suit and pearls, along the deserted waterfront back to lunch.

At this time of year such a meal at the Glenmore was merely functional. Drinks were available in the bar beforehand, in the expectation perhaps that a couple of gins might so dull the senses that lack of subtlety in the salad or flavour in the pâté would pass unnoticed. Fiona, daring a martini, found herself alone at one of the tiny white tables, the more elderly visitors either being non-drinkers on the advice of their physicians or, having come straight from morning service, considering it unseemly to imbibe intoxicants before filling their stomachs.

Fiona was still not used to being alone in such a place. There had always been Mother to gain immediate attention wherever she went, addressing staff and strangers alike in her high-pitched, well-bred voice so that she would become a centre, setting up small lines of communication that involved Fiona in the same casual social network. Now Fiona sat twiddling with the stem of her glass and stroking her handbag.

"I see you are alone, may I join you?"

It was the same man who had spoken to her at breakfast. Fiona moved her bag from the table and nodded. Would she care for another martini? She would, feeling her colour rise, and she watched him as he went over to the bar. He had the lithe tread of a leopard, soft-footed and sure of himself, but his suit was of cheap material and shiny at the back. Fiona had already marked him down as a cad. This was within the limits of her admittedly narrow perception, but even her necessarily restricted experience had taught her the lamentable truth that most of her late mother's doctrines were all too depressingly sound. Her mother would have made no bones about putting him in the catalogue as a cad.

And her mother would have been right.

TWO

To GIVE HIM his due, Fergus O'Connell himself, traveller in fancy goods and hairdressers' sundries, would have agreed with her. Indeed he'd been heard to boast in the commercial hotels he normally frequented: "I'm a bit of a cad with the ladies," accompanied by a knowing smile and a quick look round to see how the remark was taken. It didn't have to be taken too literally, for Fergus O'Connell was only a bit of a cad in the same way as he was only a bit of the owld Irish, a wee bit Scottish, a bit of a Catholic, a bit of a Protestant, a bit of an honest man—that was in his work where he was scrupulous—and a bit of a rogue.

A very partitioned man, Fergus, and as he carried the two drinks over to the white table where Fiona awaited him, an open-hearted and transient man. For he too had just been liberated by a death. This was the circumstance which had brought him in celebration to the Glenmore rather than to the Pierhead Inn where his fellow travellers foregathered.

He had read his sister Sadie's letter with a lightening of the heart: "Dear Fergus," she had written, "I went to your poor wife's funeral last week. I didn't suppose you knew she'd passed away but I felt I owed it to her. I didn't think you'd turn up anyway after all this time. She's left you the £500 in her post office savings book . . ."

He'd not seen Emily since they'd parted amicably enough some ten years past. Neither of them had bothered to get a divorce; they were both free-wheelers in that respect, yet already Fergus felt exhilarated by his changed status and some extension of his frame of mind, rising like Proteus from the sea, made him look more intently at Fiona Davison-Maclean. He saw first the crocodile handbag and matching shoes and noticed en passant that the ankles were shapely despite serviceable denier. Moving upwards the body was well-nourished, even to slight plumpness about the waist, evidence of good food and little exercise; untouched breasts bulged innocently beneath cashmere jumper and the pearls around the flushed throat were real. The face too was real, blank as an open cheque, the greenish eyes flickering nervously.

It had been her half-turned-away head which had taken his attention as he went in to breakfast. For one moment he thought... No, it couldn't be... That fleeting likeness, instantly dismissed as a trick of colouring and set of the shoulders, had made him speak to the woman as she raised her eyes and met his stare which she might have thought impertinent.

Now he saw the heavy chin and thin lips, the irregularity of feature which makes for plainness, and he wondered idly if she was as rich as her clothes seemed to indicate. Without conscious resolve he probed gently to find out.

Getting along with women was part of his daily business, now become a habit and requiring no effort. On his journeys through the Lowland shires—in or out of season made no difference, for ladies must always have their hair done—his run-of-the-mill sales of razors, strops and cutlery, setting lotions and tail combs, were easily augmented even in winter by off-loading slow-movers like diamanté Alice bands and jewelled slides—illusions of some good life in the expansive cities—once he had warmed the lonely hearts of the female proprietors—and their beds also when he had a mind to. The rewards for what was in effect the mere exercise of one facet of his nature in areas where others deemed it unprofitable to bother, were full order books to satisfy his employers and sufficient commission to keep Fergus in the style to which he had become accustomed.

Only in the last year had he become uneasy. He was over forty and although still good-looking enough to wheedle his old clients into buying new hair tints and flashy nail varnish, he was sharply aware that the younger set were into blow-drying and home-perms, and the cheeky flip girls just out of their apprenticeships and buying their own premises had no time for his jokey flirtations. He could see that the days of the journeyman were over; chemists sold the cosmetics now, and even the barbers ordered their supplies direct. Fergus had begun to worry about his future and his own thinning hair—no matter how carefully he combed it over his narrow scalp. He had no future prospects in his firm; keen younger men were treading on his tail, and at the end of it all there would be no pension—just a farewell party and find your own way home, Fergus.

Engaged now in easy conversation with Fiona while mentally stripping her assets, he too was ripe for development. With Emily's small legacy to come—he blessed her perfunctorily for that as he had crossed himself from old habit when he'd read Sadie's letter—he was in the mood for a small adventure. It need be nothing too ambitious—Fergus was not an ambitious man, nor was he reckless—but he sensed he had come to a tide in his life and he found the thought exciting. He would go where it took him.

Later that evening as they stood on the Esplanade, the waters below them came to the floodtide. Fergus accepted it as an omen of good fortune.

THREE

LENNOX KEMP was having supper with his employer, George McCready, and his lady wife in their stuffy Edwardian house in Muswell Hill. There had been a certain ambiguity about the invitation. It was not McCready's custom to entertain any of the staff of McCready's Detective Agency at his home, and Kemp could only think he had been asked because he was on the point of leaving the Agency anyway.

He had spent some six years in the wilderness, deprived—quite justly—of the privilege of practising his profession, but now the Law Society in its wisdom had re-opened its doors to him and he was once more enrolled as a solicitor of the Supreme Court and free to take up whatever appointment in law he chose. The trouble was that, according to McCready, Kemp was being too choosy: "You've had offers, laddie—your old firm would have you back, and so would that place in Hertfordshire where you helped them out on that murder case..."

All that was true enough but still Lennox Kemp hesitated. The prospect of spending his days on routine conveyancing, endless probate, the making and undoing of wills, the drafting of leases and the intricacies of tax avoidance schemes held no joy for him. As for court work, to which he had once brought enthusiasm and skill, he feared his law had grown too rusty to pursue it with the necessary cut and thrust. Glumly he considered the possibility that in fact he had no great wish to be a solicitor again, and emboldened now by Grace McCready's heavy supper and a glass or two of her husband's finest malt he voiced this doubt aloud.

"Ye're more of a fool than I thought," McCready growled. "It's high time ye got back into your profession. Get a steady job and ye'll soon settle down."

"Wheesht, now, George," Mrs. McCready admonished him. "Give Mr. Kemp time. That's all he needs. Maybe he could do with a wee holiday. You've been working him too hard down at the Agency."

Kemp turned to her in astonishment. It was well known among the operatives at McCready's that it was she who scrutinized the time-sheets, docked their expenses, complained about the size of the telephone bills, and generally saw to it that the Agency books showed considerable profits. McCready himself had been a highly-respected and competent enough police officer until his retirement and ran the business on the strength of that reputation, but it was his wife who made sure it paid.

So Kemp looked into her bright blue Scottish eyes— eyes which tended to remind him of another equally resolute lady who as a child had run about the castle of Glamis—and wondered what she was up to.

George McCready poured out another two generous helpings of straw-coloured spirit and said: "Don't worry, Lennox, ye can get a taxi home..."

Such practical consideration for his lawful well-being coming from such a source immediately made

Kemp the more suspicious. What, he asked himself, was this elderly pair of canny Scots about to require of him?

Cautiously he said: "A holiday? Now just where did you have in mind?"

McCready had a sudden fit of coughing. It could have been the whisky but Kemp didn't think so. He waited.

Grace McCready folded her plump arms across her massive chest and gave Kemp a benign look.

"Have you thought of Scotland?"

"I haven't thought of anywhere, Mrs. McCready."

"Ah well, you might well do so. It's nice up there this time of year."

Kemp doubted that. It was February.

He became aware that both the McCreadys were acting like reluctant conspirators. He'd be here till midnight if he didn't prod them along.

"Come on, out with it. You want me to do a job for you, isn't that it?"

"Not me." McCready did his best to dissociate himself from whatever disclosure was about to emerge. "It's all Grace's idea..." He left his wife to tell her tale.

"I have a niece, Mr. Kemp. She's called Fiona Davison-Maclean—that's hyphenated, ye ken, they were the monied side of the family—and I would hear from her and her mother several times in a year. I'd get a wee letter on my birthday and aye a card at Christmas, and postcards when they were on holiday. Well, her mother, that was my sister Anna, she died last October. I'd a letter from Fiona then. She didn't expect me to travel up for the funeral. It's a long way and she knows how I suffer with my arthritis, but it was a nice letter and she sent me some trinkets of her mother's—family things she thought I might like. She's a good girl, Fiona, in that way. Always very thoughtful. Not like her mother. I must tell you, Lennox—'' Kemp noticed that, like her husband, Mrs. McCready dropped easily into familiarity when she wanted something—''that I never got on with my sister, Anna. She was aye selfish, even as a girl, and she married into money. Jack Davison-Maclean came of a prosperous family, and he was in jute. Ye'll ken there was a lot of money in that during the 'twenties and 'thirties, and Jock was a good business man. He's been dead over ten year now. I'd no quarrel with him, it was only my sister that put on airs. Right snobbish she was, and me only married to a policeman.''

McCready gave a snort. "Get on with it, Grace.''

"Anyway, to get to the point, I've no' heard from Fiona since that letter in October. No Christmas card, and no word on my birthday which was last week . . .''

"When her mother died would Fiona come into all the money?'' asked Kemp.

"Oh yes, there's no one else. But that wouldn't have made any difference to Fiona. I mean she'd always had money spent on her, that's the way she was brought up. She'd be no stranger to it. She'd been sent to St. Columba's—private education, ye ken, the best in Scotland . . .'' From Grace McCready's severe tone it was obviously in her view the best in Europe also; no argument. '' . . . and after her father died she and her mother travelled all over the place, stayed at good hotels . . . They had a big house out in Bearsden—that's one of the best districts of Glasgow—and plenty of servants . . . Fiona's aye been used to money.''

"She never worked, this Fiona?''

Mrs. McCready looked shocked.

"Of course not. She looked after her mother. Was at her beck and call . . .''

"The price she paid for the expensive upbringing, no doubt,'' remarked Kemp with a hint of sardonic amusement, but Grace McCready was too far into her story to notice.

"Well, when I never had a card at Christmas I wrote again to my niece but I'd no reply. And when no word came on my birthday I phoned Bearsden. Imagine my surprise to find the house was sold! There were new people in it and they couldn't give me any address for Fiona. They'd moved in at the end of the year and they'd no idea where she was.''

Kemp turned to McCready.

"I suppose you've tried at her lawyers? What do they call them up there, writers to the signet, isn't it?''

"It was no good.'' McCready shook his head. "The firm who dealt with the sale of the house weren't the family solicitors anyway—just a Glasgow firm who dealt solely with the property. We don't know who the Davison-Maclean lawyers are—Grace has been out of Scotland for over forty years, and she's had very little to do with her sister in all that time. But Fiona was different—she always kept in touch. That is until now . . .''

Kemp sat back, and considered.

At length he said: "Mrs. McCready, if I was a girl who'd just lost her mother to whom I'd been bound hand and foot..."

"She's no girl, Fiona," interrupted Grace Mc-Cready, "she's going on forty."

"All right, if I was a woman who'd just been set free from duty and the dull domestic round, I know what I'd do...I'd hop on a plane and go round the world."

Grace McCready pounced again.

"Ah no, Fiona would not do that. Even when she was young she was aye feared to fly. She would never go on a plane. That was the reason she and her mother never travelled abroad—Anna complained of sea-sickness. And that wasn't one of her fads either—she really did get sick. I've seen my sister as a girl puking over the side of a Clyde steamer if there was the least roll between Dunoon and Wemyss Bay!"

Kemp reflected that even the rich and leisured had their problems.

"At least I'd take a trip somewhere," he went on rather lamely, "if only to have a change of scene. And your Fiona's probably done just that. Sold the house and settled somewhere else."

Mrs. McCready shook her head.

"Without a word to her aunt? No, Lennox, that's not like Fiona. She'd have sent me a change of address at the very least. I am very very worried about her."

Lennox Kemp could see from her puckered eyes that she was, although he himself didn't think the circumstances sufficiently bizarre to warrant her anxiety.

"What about the place she went to with her mother? She could have decided to stay in a hotel for a while, couldn't she? Perhaps she's simply house-hunting..."

"In Gleneagles?" Grace's scorn was blatant. "Peebles Hydro? Yon big places she and Anna made the rounds of? No, Fiona wouldn't go to them on her own."

Kemp turned to McCready helplessly.

"What do you think?"

George cleared his throat. "I do share Grace's anxiety. I've only met Fiona the few times she and her mother came to London. It would be Claridges then—Anna was quite at home there, but Fiona—" he shook his head—"I can't see her in these places on her own. She's the typical sat-on spinster daughter. Very shy. Hasn't a word to say for herself. And she's got no looks to speak of..."

His wife protested, bridling at the hint of a slur on what possibly might be a family likeness.

"She wasn't a bad-looking lass when she was younger."

"Well, she's not young now, Grace, and she's not the type to improve with age. It's been over three years since we saw her, and even then she was growing plump, dowdy and middle-aged. You thinking what I'm thinking, Lennox?"

"Maybe. Would she have much experience of men, Mrs. McCready?"

She was not slow to take the point.

"That's just what I said to George. She's fallen victim to a fortune-hunter!"

Kemp had to laugh. Victorian conventions die hard in Scottish bosoms, and her phrasing was inimitable.

"And so, dear reader, she married him..." Even Mrs. McCready smiled at Kemp's effort to cap her but she wagged a warning finger at him all the same. "I know you think I read nothing but Annie S. Swan in the *People's Friend*," she said. Kemp who had heard of neither, nevertheless grinned as she swung round and jabbed the same finger at McCready. "But I know very well what goes on in the real world, through him!"

"I can guess what you want me to do," said Kemp when the small by-play was over. "You want me to go up to Scotland and look for Fiona Davison-Maclean or whatever her name has become. That's going to be the difficult part..."

"There are marriage registers up there as well as in England—and probably better kept," said Grace tartly, but she added sugar as she went on: "Oh, Lennox, I should be so grateful if you would just find her. If she's married and happy, well, then, it doesn't really matter who she's married to. I only want to know if she's all right..."

"That she's alive," put in George McCready grimly. "Usual expenses, Lennox—in fact a damned sight better in this case. I'd like Fiona found—it'll ease my mind too if we do all we can. It shouldn't be a difficult assignment. Fiona'll no' be far away from her home, I'll be bound. Now Grace will tell you everything you want to know about her niece and the family..."

She did, and at length, so that it was long past midnight when Kemp finally left their house—by taxi. George's hospitality to further his wife's whim having extended well beyond the legal alcoholic limit.

Home in his own nondescript flat, Kemp took a look at the bundle of photographs thrust into his hand by Grace McCready. Most of them would be useless, he reflected, shifting through what were obviously early family snapshots, and even the most recent—taken some five years ago—was not helpful. Taken on some hotel terrace in full sun, it showed Anna Davison-Maclean as the dominant figure, a handsome old lady fashionably overdressed. Beside her Fiona's face was blurred and out of focus but there was no hiding the fact that she was plain with a straight uncompromising hairstyle that only emphasized the heavy features, and that she had already much of Grace McCready's bulkiness of figure—an unattractive combination for a woman in her thirties.

Ah well, thought Kemp, she has the money. You can't have everything in this life.

FOUR

FERGUS O'CONNELL drove his new Mercedes off the car ferry at Rothesay and gave the seamen operating the gangplank his customary cheery wave, purely out of habit for he was in no mood for bonhomie. They knew him from other days, of course, when he trundled ashore in his old Austin, the backseat piled high with samples. Aye, and they'd have known then where he would be going straight off the pier—up to Lisa Ferguson's wee salon on Montague Street. But not this time. Now he headed out along the West Road to the renovated farmhouse by the loch. He and Fiona had bought the place outright—to the surprise of the Bute Estates who normally only rented it to families from the South up for the shooting, or the fishing on Loch Aline. It was Fiona who insisted on buying the feu, even at what seemed to Fergus's canny soul an extortionate asking price.

"I want a base," she had said, "I've always had a base. We can travel about if you want to, Fergus, but we must always have a home to return to."

He hadn't argued with her. It would be pointless to do so while she still held the purse-strings. Since he'd thrown up his job in the first euphoria of the marriage—that too had been at Fiona's suggestion—Fergus had slowly become aware of his financial dependence on her. During their brief courtship he had looked no further forward than the actual wedding day. To find that this pale, plumpish woman on the edge of middle-age was such an easy pushover had at first delighted him, then thrown him into a kind of benign coma. On learning how rich she was—Fergus was no fool when it came to interpreting legal documents and stock-holdings—he felt as though battered about the head by good fortune. He'd never been a deep-thinking man, taken life as it came, ducked any issue which looked serious, and preferred the surface of things so long as they were pleasurable and made no demands on him. He had spent Emily's savings quite consciously on making himself a presentable suitor, from underwear to topcoat, discarding old clothes and indulging in expensive shoes and other accoutrements—not only to impress but also because he was vain and would readily admit to it.

They had been married some three months, and still he felt bemused and obscurely uneasy. He had plunged headlong into deep waters and was only now striking out for the shores of reality. Perhaps it was the same for Fiona, but as he had never considered any woman's feelings beyond the stage of their succumbing to his flattery and come-as-you-go conquest the thought went no further. He had been mildly shocked by her inept passion; it seemed to him at odds with her upbringing about which she was vigorously talkative. Such passion did not fit his concept of her as a person of education and class. Had he been inclined to introspection—which he was not—he might have reflected that hitherto the only woman with whom he had had any close relationship was his mother, a devout Catholic long dead but still holding for him the image both of the Virgin Mary and patient Griselda. Emily in that respect had never counted, being, like himself, a creature of easygoing virtue and natural mutability.

That Fiona had married him in a desperate fling of late romantic yearning, the spinster's last hope, he was quite willing to allow. "If ye marry a single woman at forty she'll aye be grateful!" one of his colleagues had gibed, half-enviously, at his office send-off party, and Fergus had laughed, well-pleased, warming to the truth as he saw it.

But was she that grateful? He spun the wheel of the new car to avoid the potholes in the track down to Lochaline House. The car she'd bought for him, certainly, but it was in her name. And the house was hers; she'd seen to that. Money was beginning to worry him—that, and other things. Passionate she was in bed but he'd had to teach her the rudiments of sex; in some ways she was like a child, a spoilt child, a demanding child. If he didn't respond, she went cold as a stone. There was none of the jolly, frolicsome love-making he was used to, and she bit her nails and looked blank at his jokes. Life with Fiona was no bed of roses despite the cushioning of money—her money.

He saw her now come to the door as he swung the car round in the drive under the clump of firs, their branches tossing and groaning in the winter gale which swept across the grey waters of the loch behind the house.

With a momentary pang of guilt he wished that it was Lisa Ferguson waiting there on the step for his re-

turn. He tried to brush the thought from him. He'd
have to watch that one. Time enough when Fiona settled down a bit. Fergus had no intention of giving up
for ever on his old ways; a man's nature goes deep, he
told himself, and it was something his wife would have
to come to terms with. She seemed to think she'd taken
possession of him like the furniture she'd bought, the
house, that blasted little yacht of hers. She has a terrible sense of property, that's her trouble, his mind
raged. It's the way she's been brought up. They store
things away, these upper-class people, they don't enjoy them, they buy houses to put things in, they buy
stocks and shares to put in the bank and watch them
grow, they don't value the things they acquire except
in money terms. Did Fiona think she had bought him?
Fergus in his capacity as a rep, and a good rep at that,
had never had political leanings one way or the other,
in the easy camaraderie of pubs and shops he'd never
found it paid; now he found himself the victim of a
growing resentment. For there was nothing easygoing
about Fiona's politics; there she stood, four-square,
wrapped in the absolute rightness of all her conservative forebears, and would brook no deviation.

And there she stood now waiting for him in the grey
stone porch, a solid figure in a good tweed suit with
the pearls at her neck. Fergus sighed, and went in with
her.

FIVE

FOR ONCE Lennox Kemp didn't know where his starting-point should be. Usually by this time he would have had some plan in mind, would have charted a line no matter how oblique that had some bearing on the object of his search. Now he saw himself working in a vacuum, a situation he deplored both as a lawyer—for they starve if not fed on facts—and as an investigator, for inquiry agents likewise demand at least an initial rope-end to grasp before swinging into the void. The void before him as he checked in at the second-class Glasgow hotel—since he had no wish at this early stage to take too much advantage of George Mc-Cready—seemed to have neither rope-holds nor hand-rails. Kemp's ignorance of the Scottish legal system was only equalled by McCready's inability to make any contacts within the local fiduciary. His fiscal world was bounded by the area covered by the Metropolitan police, with some old friends within the limits of the home counties. To both of them Scotland was an alien land.

Kemp slung down his paltry luggage and considered his next move—but not over-seriously. He regarded this trip to the North as no more than that. McCready's Agency was paying for a whim on the part of his employer's wife.

But Grace McCready was already wrong on one count: February in Scotland was not nice. The weather was appalling; east winds sweeping across the North Sea from the Siberian steppes had cleared the streets of people as Kemp drove into the city. These same icy winds had brought curtains of sleet down across the dismal tenements, and were even now slashing at the hotel windows. The curse of Scotland, thought Kemp bitterly before he finally slept, adjusting his podgy form into the lumps of the mattress.

As he drove out the next morning to Bearsden that east wind was still blowing, dry now of sleet but keen as a knife-edge where it made contact with shivering flesh. Kemp, not normally susceptible to weather, was irritated to find himself spluttering and coughing. Jesus, what a country! How on earth had the honeyed Mary fresh from the warm fields of France ever survived in this desolate land? How was he, Lennox Kemp, ever to survive?

Drawing up outside the solid stone house—it might well be called a mansion except that all the others in this secluded drive were of similar size—he got out and pulled his coat collar round his face to protect it from the wintry blast. "Briardene" said the incised lettering on the gatepost. No good calling there, it had been sold to strangers, but Grace McCready had mentioned neighbours, the Langmuirs at "Invermead" next door.

The bell, pulled by a jangling chain, was quaint and old-fashioned and so was the appearance of the parlourmaid who answered it. She showed Kemp through the glass-walled vestibule and draughty hall into a small cosy sitting-room wherein sat Mr. and Mrs. Langmuir and their married daughter, Alison Teviot, a smartly-dressed handsome woman in her early forties. It was she who rose and greeted him, her parents remaining seated as in a family portrait, their bottoms firmly held by velvet chairs on either side of the fireplace.

"You are the gentleman who rang this morning?"

"I'm Lennox Kemp. It's good of you to see me."

She gestured him to the sofa, and inquired if he would take tea or coffee.

"Tea, please. No sugar." He forestalled the question. "I understand you knew Mrs. Davison-Maclean and her daughter?"

Alison Teviot tinkled china and spoons, handed cups and saucers carefully while the elderly couple stayed straight-backed, silent and almost immobile. It was clear they did not intend to say anything until their buttons were pressed.

"Fiona Davison-Maclean's aunt in London is anxious to have news of her," said Kemp by way of openers. "Have you any idea where she can be reached?"

"I'm sorry, but I've not seen Fiona nor heard from her since the day of the funeral. That would be in October, wasn't it, Mother?"

Mrs. Langmuir merely nodded.

"You mean she left right away?"

"It would seem so. She told me she thought of taking a short holiday. It would be the natural thing."

"A short holiday? She said that?"

"Yes. Then quite suddenly—it must have been just over a month later—Briardene was put up for sale."

"She didn't come back? Surely she must have, if only to see to her own belongings?"

"She may have done so. I certainly didn't see her. But I would be at home in Edinburgh, of course... Did you see Fiona, Mother? Did she come back to Briardene?" From her raised voice and precise articulation Kemp guessed that Mrs. Langmuir was slightly deaf. She now inclined her head, fragile as a harebell on a stalk, but her voice was firm enough.

"Fiona came once at the beginning of November. Is that not so Edward?"

When the old gentleman replied it was in a gentle reminiscent tone as if reciting half-forgotten poetry.

"I saw her in the garden. I remember talking about the mildness of the autumn. She said the gardener must sweep the leaves from the lawn and tidy the flower-beds. I agreed. Her mother had been most particular about the treatment of her roses before the winter set in. When I mentioned this to Fiona she said that was not the reason but she merely wanted things straight because she was selling the house. I said, you must not be hasty, you must think carefully... That's what I said to her, wasn't it, Mother?"

Mrs. Langmuir made a stiff movement of her neck in agreement.

"But she went ahead and sold, Mr. Kemp," Alison said. "I believe she did come in and say goodbye to Mother and Father before she went..."

Mr. Langmuir was not deaf.

"She came at the end of that week. Said she would not be back. It was civil of her to call but I told her she had made too sudden a decision... I told her not to be so hasty. But she didn't listen to me..."

"Did she say where she was going to live?" Kemp leant forward eagerly.

"It was not my business to ask," said Mr. Langmuir reprovingly, "since she had made no move to tell us."

"You see, we didn't know the Davison-Macleans all that well," Alison said hurriedly, "although they'd been our neighbours for years and I'd grown up with Fiona. After Mr. Davison-Maclean died they hadn't been too friendly—" she lowered her voice—"well, I suppose it was Fiona's mother really. She was not easy to get on with. Anyway, I'd married and gone away. I'm actually only visiting now. My home is in Edinburgh but I come as often as I can to see my parents. I'm sorry I can't help you as to Fiona's whereabouts. We'd drifted apart."

"Were you surprised she sold up?"

"Not really. I don't suppose her life with her mother had been very happy. I can understand her wanting to get away, but to make a decision like that, in such a hurry, no, that wasn't like the Fiona I knew."

"Do you think she might have met someone?"

Surprisingly, it was Mr. Langmuir who answered. He was quite an astute old gentleman and not really as mummified as he looked.

"That is what I think happened," he said now in his singsong voice. "She met some fellow. There are fellows like that about, you know. Fellows who would take advantage. She would be very rich now, Fiona.

Wouldn't you say so, Mother? Wouldn't Fiona be very rich?"

His wife nodded vigorously. Her voice quavered, clear and slightly cracked like the bell at their door.

"Fiona had never been sought after. Her mother often said so..."

Kemp looked inquiringly at Alison Teviot. She made a small grimace. "I'm afraid it was true, Mr. Kemp. Mrs. Davison-Maclean had been very good-looking in her day, I suppose. Anyway, she did rather take it out on Fiona that she wasn't attractive."

"And wasn't she?"

"Well, I'm afraid that when we were all young together round here we called Fiona 'pudding-face'—and we thought we had good reason. She went away to school eventually—she didn't go to the local Girls' High like the rest of us—so that when she came back she didn't have many friends, certainly no boy-friends. And I'm afraid her looks weren't the type to improve—she was still an awkward, rather lumpy girl."

"The roses were in her cheeks that day," Mr. Langmuir said suddenly.

"What day was that, Father?"

"When she came about clearing the garden," he rejoined impatiently. "What day d'you think I meant? The funeral? She was a poor white-faced thing then and not helped by that young man's yammering. That long-haired puppy..."

Kemp raised an eyebrow inquiringly at Alison Teviot.

"Father must mean Fiona's cousin, Lindsay Davison-Maclean. He does wear his hair rather in the fashion." She kept her voice low. "Father took a dislike to him at the funeral because Lindsay laughed at Fiona's hat." She couldn't repress a smile. "I'm sorry, but it was rather terrible. Lindsay said it looked like one of these sacks coal-heavers used to put over their heads. Anyway, Fiona heard him and she was furious."

Kemp had done his homework on the Davison-Maclean Edinburgh connection. "Lindŝay Davison-Maclean is Fiona's only relative—apart from her aunt, Grace McCready, isn't that so?"

"I've never really thought about it but I suppose he is. His father would have been Fiona's uncle, and I know that he is dead and so's his mother, and Lindsay is an only child just like Fiona..." Mrs. Teviot looked somewhat startled at the path her thoughts had taken.

Kemp smiled across at Mr. Langmuir and remarked in an easy tone, "You said she had the roses in her cheeks. It was November—did you mean she was sunburned?"

The old gentleman's glance was withering.

"I meant what I said, young man."

Kemp grinned. It was warming, even in this chill country to be so addressed. "Your father is a most perceptive man, Mrs. Teviot."

She looked pleased but bewildered.

"He says Fiona looked a poor thing at the funeral," went on Kemp, "white-faced, he called her. Was she always of a pallid complexion?"

"I'm afraid so. Rather pasty, it was, and she had eyes a bit like green gooseberries... I'm afraid I've made her sound rather unattractive. That thick pale skin was, I believe, considered modish in Edwardian times when they called it magnolia, but of course it's out of fashion now when colour is everything." Alison touched her own fresh cheek which was rosy enough. "And Fiona hated make-up so that she always looked somewhat drab..."

"Yet in November a month after the funeral the roses were there?" Again Kemp smiled across at Edward Langmuir. "And if it wasn't make-up then it meant that she was happy?"

The old man looked smug and sat back with an air of triumph. "That's just what I meant. Didn't I say so at the time, Edith?" But his wife was half-asleep and made no response.

"I see what you're getting at, Mr. Kemp," Alison said with a measure of disbelief. "You think she met someone. Well, it certainly was no one from round here. We would have known. We have the social contacts."

Kemp could well believe it although he would have termed it differently; the place would be a minefield of gossip. Even if the elderly retired were restricted in their movements their parlourmaids and cooks would see to it that material was not lacking.

"I'm afraid I'm tiring your parents," said Kemp, rising. "Besides, I think I must pay a visit to Edinburgh and have a word with Fiona's cousin. What does he do?"

"Not a great deal. He was left fairly well-off, and he drifts. I think he mentioned at the funeral that he was taking Law at the University but I shouldn't think for a moment he's serious about it. He must be well over thirty."

She did not summon the parlourmaid but showed Kemp to the door herself. "You don't like Cousin Lindsay, do you?" Kemp said to her as they stood in the draughty hall. Alison Teviot was flustered by so direct an inquiry but did her best to answer as honestly as her habitual good manners allowed.

"I think I agree with Father. Lindsay's behaviour at the funeral was unnecessarily flippant. He could at least have pretended sympathy—it is the custom, you know. But of course you must judge for yourself when you meet him..." For a prudent matron she felt she might have gone too far in censure. "Perhaps you would care to take my own Edinburgh address, Mr. Kemp. I too would be interested to know that Fiona is well—and—er..."

"Happy?"

"I hope so. I do really. She ought to get something more out of life. Do you know, I don't think I ever saw her happy? Oh, yes, once. Her father had a yacht years ago on the Clyde, and when Fiona would be about twelve he began to teach her to sail. All that summer they spent days on the water, and I remember she looked quite different—really alive for the first time, in her rather gauche way. The same thing happened when she took up tennis. There had been a court at Briardene then—her father had been a good player and he taught Fiona... Looking back now, I think she had the makings of a fair athlete. I remember the odd times I played with her she had a really powerful service, and she took her game very seriously. She was quite strong, you know... But of course her mother wasn't keen on that kind of thing—Fiona's playing wasn't ladylike, she said. Anyway the tennis didn't last—the court was made into flowerbeds, and by the time Fiona went off to school her father had begun to travel more on business, and he gave up the yacht. Mrs. Davison-Maclean hated boats—so there was no more sailing either for Fiona... Seems a pity, now... Yes, Mr. Kemp, please do let me know when you trace Fiona's whereabouts..."

She regrets that epithet "pudding-face," Kemp reflected as he crunched his way down the drive. After all these years perhaps it had come home to Alison Teviot that she had not been kind to the girl next door who had carried her plain looks like a birthmark, and that it might now be too late to make amends.

SIX

TWENTY-SEVEN BELLVIEW TERRACE was the address in the Edinburgh telephone directory for the only Davison-Maclean. L. for the Lindsay who had laughed at Fiona's funeral hat. The district was Morningside, very sedate; tall houses like rows of Presbyterian elders, grand dignified flats, self-contained, complacent like the folk they housed who would live well-conducted lives within their privacy. Kemp crossed a quiet square after parking his car. Early shoppers were hurrying out, middle-class matrons in sensible shoes, as sure of their foothold on the earth as of their eventual place in heaven.

There had been no reply to his telephone call so Kemp had decided on a visit. He rang the bell which gave a good stirring modern sound. And equally modern and stirring in a different sense was the girl who opened the door. He took in her clothes first—they impinged somehow upon his inward eye as though he had once seen her in a dream: scarlet satin tunic, black velvet pants, a gold chain slung low on her hips. She stood looking at him with dark insolent eyes, a cigarette held between two red-tipped fingers in an exaggerated gesture of nonchalance—just possibly not contrived. She said nothing, merely arched thin eyebrows.

"I was looking for Lindsay Davison-Maclean?"

"You came to the right place. Come in."

There was a spacious hall, plain polished parquet floor, one glowing Persian rug square in the centre. The sitting-room was large, given grandeur by high ceiling and lofty windows, but it was warm and inviting. Low comfortable chairs, a sofa, a few handsome pieces of antique furniture set against pale Adam green walls or islanded upon the apricot Chinese washed carpet were evidence of an expensive taste expensively indulged.

"Drink or coffee, Mr.—er—?"

"Lennox Kemp. I wouldn't mind a whisky. Your Edinburgh winds are murder."

Without further comment she poured amber fluid into squat crystal tumblers, passed a siphon and a jug of water. Her movements were graceful, and without fuss.

She came and perched on an arm of the sofa. "I'm sorry Lindsay is out. Will I do?"

Kemp laughed. The whisky took his throat in a warm loving embrace. It was the first time he'd felt like laughing since coming to the North.

"And you are . . . ?"

"His mistress." She gave a small bow. "An old-fashioned term, but for want of a better . . . Alexina Angus. You can call me Alex, most people do."

"All right, Alex. When will he be back?"

She shrugged, dislodging the red satin from one white shoulder and lower. Kemp blinked. It was only eleven in the morning, and this was supposed to be a cold city, this Athens of the North, exquisite Dunedin, home of rational thought.

"I've no idea when Lindsay will return. He goes his way, I go mine. What about another drink?"

Kemp settled back, relaxed, and accepted. After all, the weather in the streets was terrible. "I wanted to see your friend Lindsay about his cousin, Fiona Davison-Maclean."

"The one with the money?"

"Yes. Does he know where she is?"

Alexina had eyes that were almost black. So was the hair pushed up on the top of her small skull and cut short into cherub curls stretching the white skin on her forehead so that she looked in a state of perpetual surprise.

"What Lindsay knows, Lindsay doesn't always tell. What's your interest, Lennox?"

"Let's just say I'm investigating."

She had a wide mouth and a devastatingly short upper lip over neat white teeth. An exotic creature to find in this stone-grey suburb. Her accent was only faintly Scottish, flattish on the vowels and a nice burr to the r's, an educated voice but lacking the higher pitch and drawl of a Southern girl.

"That's a pretty name, Alexina. Where did you get it?"

She leaned forward to flick ash from her cigarette. The slippery folds of her blouse were fluid across her bosom without underlying constriction, and the little hills and valleys thus defined looked deserving of an affectionate pat.

"My mother was Highland," she said, accepting his glance as no more than her due, "and they always wanted sons. If there were daughters they sublimated their aspirations and compromised. I come from a long line of Williaminas, Davidinas, and Thomasinas. Women's lib has been slow to reach the Western Isles.''

Kemp hurriedly amended his opinion of her. Not only a dish of sweets but articulate withal. Over the edge of her glass her black eyes laughed at him.

''You're English,'' she said, ''you think modern ideas stop at Watford.''

He raised his own glass to her.

''I'm only learning,'' he said.

She slipped down on to the sofa and stretched her long legs, small toes upturned in bronze ballet slippers.

''So, you are on the trail of the vanished Fiona?''

''Who said she'd vanished?''

''Lindsay is looking for her too.''

''Is he now. And why would that be?''

Her mouth curled in a gamine grin but her eyes remained shrewd.

''You tell me, Mr. Lennox Kemp from England.''

''Because of the money?''

''What else?''

''But Lindsay surely has enough... Look at this place.''

''Haven't you ever noticed that the rich always want to be richer?''

Kemp ignored the rhetorical question and asked a more pertinent one of his own. ''And how far has Lindsay got?''

''How far have you got?'' she countered, rising and taking his glass. My God, thought Kemp hazily, they drink fast in Edinburgh. It can't just be the weather. Yet the contrast between the chill outside where even the scattered leaves and paper bags at street corners seemed not so much blown about by the wind as begging the breeze to lift them in charity from the frozen pavements, and the warm luxury of the flat was striking. Something of this sense of contrast permeated his mind—already lulled into seeking universal truths by the rising warmth of the whisky. Could this polarization of the elements explain the North's dark history? He had already been thinking of that Queen coming to this threadbare land, the fanaticism of its inhabitants, their need for, and their hatred of, the beauty and silken dalliance she brought; the beguiling music they had cut short so sharply on that bloodstained narrow stair; had it reached her soul too, the contrast of light and dark, that terrible night at Kirk o' Field?

Kemp would have admitted to anyone that his mind was confused by the generous measures poured by Alex. He remembered the Langmuirs, upright in their puritan consciences, secure in the solid worth of their draughty mansion; he sensed the closed-mouth bigotry behind the gaunt tenements glimpsed in the back streets of both cities; all these things were alien to his Southern temperament, the easygoing ways of the English, but he guessed he would have to come to terms with them in whatever investigation lay ahead.

Struggling to gain some control over these incoherent thoughts, nevertheless he reached out for his replenished glass.

"Have you ever met Fiona?" he asked, eying the amber fluid now with respect.

"No," she answered, "I've never met Lindsay's cousin." She dropped into the vernacular. "She widnae be o' the same class, ye ken. She belongs tae the unco' guid. She'd hae naethin' to dae wi' the likes o' me..."

Kemp grinned, and was not to be taken in.

"I'm an expert in that particular field, Miss Alexina Angus, and you defy such inept classification."

She lit a cigarette, offering him none, and lighting her own with a small gold lighter, a flash of diamond at its centre. "Touché," she remarked complacently, pulling up the satin neckline of her tunic. "We all make mistakes. But, seriously, I'm as interested as you are in the whereabouts of Fiona Davison-Maclean. I have my own theory—as Lindsay has."

"And your theory is?"

"What is yours, Lennox Kemp?"

"That she has met a man," said Kemp carefully, "that she has taken off with him, possibly married him, and gone to earth some place in connubial bliss."

"Lindsay thinks the same. Well, the first part anyway. He would have doubts about any hope of bliss for Fiona, and after all he knows her, and we don't..."

They were interrupted by the slamming of the outer door. Kemp sat up straight and tried to look like an intelligent investigator. Alexina didn't move.

THE MAN who came in looked younger than his thirty-five years. He had a pale, slightly freckled complexion, gingery-brown hair elegantly long but expertly styled, and his grey corduroy suit was conservative enough to have been worn by a clergyman in mufti.

Lindsay Davison-Maclean, however, bore no other resemblance to a man of the church; indeed, by his swaggering manner and colourful mode of speech—albeit in the rather prim Edinburgh accent—he obviously thought himself something of a dog. To Kemp his appearance seemed not unlike that of those obscure eighteenth-century gentlemen depicted in portrait galleries, hauteur in their eyes, superiority in their stance. It remained to be seen whether he shared their aristocratic stupidity.

After introductions he and Kemp got down to some polite verbal sparring—the game strangers play to fix bearings, assess status and generally "place" each other. Lindsay digested Kemp's prosaic background—grammar school education and law degree from King's College, London—without comment but was impressed by his being a solicitor.

"I might just scrape through the BL here in Edinburgh," he remarked, flipping his university tie, "but I'll be damned if I could be bothered doin' the whole stint. Bloody bore, all these exams..."

Kemp for his part took in Lindsay's Fettes education, the subsequent pecking at various careers interspersed with world trips, shooting, fishing and other pursuits agreeable to a wealthy dilettante. Lindsay was certainly not a sticker at anything. By now going easy on the whisky, Kemp brooded on the unused talents of the children of the rich, and decided that although this scion of the Davison-Macleans might play the fool, that was no reason to take him at face value.

Coming down to brass tacks, he said: "Do you really think your cousin has disappeared deliberately?"

"Yep. She's gone and married a man of a lower caste who's picked her off the shelf and dusted her down."

"Then why didn't she write and tell her aunt?"

"Good old Grace McCready, spouse to flat-footed George? Fiona'd be too ashamed . . ."

Lennox forbore to mention that McCready had been a noted athlete in his day; Lindsay's airy dismissal of him sounded like inbuilt family prejudice.

"Ashamed?"

"Well, if you knew Fiona as I know Fiona," crooned her cousin, "you wouldn't ask. Any man who plucked her out of her spinsterhood must be a man to be ashamed of. He would only do it for the money."

Kinship north of the border didn't seem to breed much kindliness. Kemp was beginning to dislike this belated student of Scottish law. The words of an old Jacobite song half-remembered were nagging at the back of his mind as, despite his protests, his glass was re-filled by his host.

And you shall drink freely the dew of Glen Sheerly,
That stream in the starlight that kings dinna ken . . .

How did that damned refrain go?

Come o'er the stream, Charlie, dear Charlie,
brave Charlie,
Come o'er the stream, Charlie,
And dine wi' Maclean...

Was that what he, Kemp, was being taken for, another Charlie?

Alexina, who had been quiet, suddenly spoke: "You sound bloody sure of yourself, Lindsay. You've found out something."

He raised a scant sandy eyebrow at her. "And what if I have?"

"I know now where you went this morning. You went to look at the marriage records!"

"An admirable system. I recommend it to you, Mr. Kemp."

"I had thought of it. Give me time..."

"Then I can save you the trouble." Lindsay's light blue eyes were full of triumphant malice. He put down his glass, dug into his breast pocket and produced a folded slip of paper. He flourished it but made no protest when Alex snatched it from him.

"You've even got a copy! You clever old Lindsay... Let's see what it says."

She read it out to them: "Fiona Lesley Davison-Maclean of Briardene, etcetera, to Fergus O'Connell of 17 Garnethill Street, Glasgow, traveller. Traveller! My God, we were right!"

Her eyes sparkled with mischief. Kemp held out his hand for the paper and read it for himself. "Dated 10th November last year. Marriage recorded in Glasgow. H'm. And all we've got is this fellow's address.''

"Some address!" Alex scoffed. "It's well seen you don't know Glasgow. Garnethill Street—up by the Art College. It'll be a cheap lodging-house, I'll bet."

"Well, you know your own slums, Lexie dear," said Lindsay amiably.

"How very dated you are. There aren't any slums nowadays—they're deprived areas where they eat people like you. They'd have you mugged in no time and stripped down to your hub-caps... But to get back to your cousin, surely this marriage puts paid to the notion you have nurtured all these years that you would come into her fortune, my sweet." It was said with some satisfaction but without animosity.

Lindsay only shrugged, and turned to Kemp.

"And what does our lawyer friend here say about that?"

"If Scottish law is the same as English in this respect—which I doubt since you follow an alien system—then if she were to die intestate her new husband would certainly reap some benefit, the statutory limit in fact, since there's unlikely to be any issue, given Fiona's age, but the residue would fall..."

"Into my lap!" chortled Lindsay. "It would be up the old paternal ancestors again!" He rolled about in laughter, relishing the phrase.

"You really are a bastard," remarked Alexina kindly. "But if this Fergus married her for her money he'd take good care she makes a will leaving him everything. Have you thought of that?"

Lindsay smirked, tapping a finger on the side of his highbridged nose. "Your Lindsay thinks of everything. You don't catch me out. Where else have I been this day?"

A sullen look came over Alex's features. "Oho... That Maggie Muir. You've been to McLintock's."

"Are they the Davison-Maclean lawyers?" Kemp said it sharply; he was feeling redundant already.

"They are indeed. Have been since way back in the dark ages. As decent an Edinburgh firm as you'd find in the New Town—and about as communicative as a closed-down cemetery. Never would they breathe a word of their clients' affairs even to their nearest and dearest... Well, especially not to their nearest and dearest."

"But you can get anything you like out of that trollop, Maggie Muir."

"Wheesht now, Lexie, don't you be calling the kettle black. I cultivate Miss Margaret Muir from the purest motives."

"I gather this lady is—what? Confidential secretary?" Kemp well knew how much information could be gleaned from such a source, although in his personal capacity he had always tried to keep to some kind of ethic. Chivalry, he felt, watching Lindsay's self-satisfied face, might well be dead in Scotland—if it had ever managed to flourish at all in this bleak land.

Unconcerned by the scrutiny, Davison-Maclean reached for the decanter and primed his drink.

"Miss Maggie told all. She's never liked Fiona—preferred dear Aunt Anna who used to buy her chocolates—and so she took an interest, shall we say? Apparently the marriage of Fiona came as a great shock to old McLintock, he's been sitting like a broody hen on the nest-egg of the Davison-Maclean fortune for years, and his interview with Fiona must have been the stuff of which epics are made . . ."

"Oh, get to the point, Lindsay. What did you wheedle out of Maggie?"

"Well," Lindsay drawled, "she was no fly on the wall, but there have to be letters, documents, papers to be typed and copied. McLintock impressed upon Fiona the importance of making a will since the marriage would invalidate any she had made previously, and I'll bet he stressed how disastrous it would be if the money went to a comparative stranger . . . But all to no avail. Our newly-wed Fiona refused his advice and no will was even drafted. More to the point, she left McLintock with no address save that of her usual bank, the Clydesdale Head Office in Glasgow, through whom all further business is to be transacted."

"So we still don't know where she is," observed Kemp. "Do you propose carrying on looking for her?"

"I fear not. I've neither the energy nor the inclination to go hunting after her now she's been stupid enough to get married, and I've certainly no wish to meet this cad who's her husband. Bound to be a cad, old chap. I'll just have to await events, won't I?" Lindsay's dismissal of the matter might be typical—from his record he was no sustainer of effort—yet Kemp did not entirely believe him. Lindsay would keep tabs on Fiona and her fortune; the knowledgeable Miss Muir would not go unvisited in the future.

Alexina sprang up. "Stay to lunch, Lennox Kemp. It's a foul day, and Lindsay does have some rather good wine."

Lindsay added his own pressure; he seemed to have taken a liking to Kemp, a feeling not altogether reciprocated, but Kemp accepted their invitation. He knew he would not be a safe driver had he attempted the journey back to Glasgow in his present state; besides, Alexina intrigued him. He had learned she was a sociology student. "What else?" she observed sardonically, "The proper study of mankind is man."

She also proved a competent cook, and the seafood concoction she laid before the men, washed down with excellent wine, was a skilful example of the effect of the Auld Alliance—if leaning more towards France than her native land. To Kemp's compliments she only replied: "What did you think we ate up here? Tatties an' herrin'?"

It turned into quite a party. It was a long time since Kemp had enjoyed himself so much. There was a lot of hilarity, and some fairly hard-edged banter.

"You put me in mind of Hammett's Continental Op," remarked Lindsay skittishly at one point, and only a degree away from insult. "Short, fat and forty."

"And you," said Kemp by way of rejoinder, "remind me of Bonnie Prince Charlie—" Alex giggled, guessing what was coming—"in his sodden, dissolute later years, of course," finished Kemp.

Lindsay rolled about with laughter, and seemed to bear no malice. "To the King over the Water, then." They drank the toast, and Alex proposed another: "To Mr. and Mrs. Fergus O'Connell—may they each get what they want..."

"Make it what they deserve," growled Lindsay, "and I'll drink to that..."

Finally it was the girl who hauled Kemp to his feet. "Come on, let's get you sobered up. A walk over the Braid Hills should do it."

There was snow on the Pentlands and a strong wind blowing. Kemp was amazed at his two companions striding out over the short springy turf, and tried to keep up with them. It gave him another insight into their characters that they were unaffected by the bitterness of the weather, but at the end of some two hours he was sharing their exhilaration as his brain cleared and he began to relish the crispness of the air and the long views.

They came down at last through the blue-grey streets as the lamps were flickering on and folks were hurrying home to warm firesides. Alex made strong coffee and they ate hot pancakes and scones dripping with butter.

Only then did they return to the subject of Fiona.

"What will you do now, Lennox?" Lindsay asked.

"Go back to London I suppose. Tell Mrs. Mc-Cready that her niece is married. She can always write to her through the Clydesdale Bank... I'm obliged to you, Lindsay, for doing my work for me."

"That's all right, old cock. I didn't do it for you. Only to satisfy my own curiosity."

It was Alexina who came out on the landing when Kemp was leaving.

"Will we see you again?" she asked, leaning on the door jamb, her black eyes sparky, her colour high. "Or rather, shall I see you again?"

Kemp kissed the end of her nose. "I hope so, Alexina Angus. Come to London." He gave her his card which she slipped into her pants pocket without looking at it. She practised the same economy of movement as of speech. "You'll be back in Scotland," she said, laughing at him, and shut the door in his face.

SEVEN

DESPITE WHAT HE HAD SAID to Lindsay and Alexina in Edinburgh Lennox Kemp had no intention of returning to London immediately; he despised an unfinished job of work.

Dinner at his hotel was supportive rather than of haute cuisine but the girl at reception was friendly and helpful when he asked for Garnethill Street.

"It's only just round the corner. Mind how you go—it's a bit steep."

He went out into the black night. The wind had dropped and a dismal icy rain was falling with the odd flutter of snowflakes half-inclined to lie on the pavement slabs. The girl had been right; Garnethill Street was a slippery trap for the unwary.

Near the top he found No. 17—one of two ground-floor flats just in off the street, the close-mouth ill-lit, smelling of damp stone, coal dust and cats.

Mrs. Lambie was courteous enough, however, and when Kemp said he was looking for Mr. O'Connell she opened the heavy door wider and asked him in. Lennox wiped his muddy feet carefully on the mat for he could see that the linoleum in the tiny hall was scrubbed clean.

"Into the kitchen with you, Mr. Kemp. I've no' a fire in the parlour."

She drew out a chair at the table where she had been sewing. A television set blinked in the corner. The nine o'clock news was on. Mrs. Lambie went over and switched it off.

Kemp again apologized for the lateness of his call; business had brought him to Glasgow and he'd hoped to see Mr. O'Connell before leaving in the morning.

"But he's no' been here since the year's end! He's got married, you know. That would be in November. He only came by about Christmastime to get the rest o' his things, and collect his mail."

"I'm sorry, Mrs. Lambie, this was the only address I had."

"Ah, you'll be one of his traveller friends?"

Kemp nodded.

"Are you with Grigson's, then?"

"No, I'm with another firm. Had Mr. O'Connell lodged with you for some time?"

"Mercy me! Fergus has been wi' me over ten years. And niver a cross word between us. Always civil-spoken he was, and fond o' a joke. Paid up prompt and niver mean wi' a bit gift when he'd the good commission. Grigson's were sorry to see him go, I'll tell ye."

"Is that Grigson's of Glasgow?" Kemp was feeling his way.

"Course it is. Down in Bothwell Street. Hairdressers' sundriesmen. You don't know much, Mr. Kemp, do you?" She was looking at him shrewdly.

Kemp quickly improvised.

"Well, my region is definitely south of the border. The firm I'm with are looking for experienced travellers to open up the Glasgow area."

Mrs. Lambie looked sceptical.

"I'd have thought Fergus O'Connell rather ould for a new job. He'd have stuck with Grigson's till he retired had he no' got married. But then, she's got money, ye ken. That's what he said tae me. Mrs. Lambie, he says, I've fallen on my feet, I'm off to lead the life o' Riley... I thocht at first it was just a joke, like, but he was serious. Threw up his job, he did, after all these years..."

"Have you an address where I could reach him?"

"He didna leave any address wi' me. And there's been no mail come for him since Christmas so he must have made other arrangements. He told me then that he and his wife hadna settled on whaur they'd live..."

Kemp looked resigned, and felt rather hopeless.

Something in his dejected attitude, huddled in his overcoat like a downcast teddy-bear, softened her suspicions or it may have been her inherent Scottish desire to be helpful to a stranger.

"I've his sister's address somewhere. She's down in England but she came to see him once, and she left me her address. I think she thought I'd a mind to keep an eye on him—in case he got ill or anything..." Mrs. Lambie got up and went over to a small bureau and produced an address book. "Here it is: Mrs. Sadie Brown, 8 Seaview Road, Southend."

Kemp made a note, thanked Mrs. Lambie for her kindness to him, and left. Perhaps the visit had not been entirely unfruitful.

Later, he telephoned the house in Muswell Hill and spoke to George McCready.

"Break the news gently to your wife. Fiona's got herself married."

Kemp gave his report fully, leaving nothing out except his own personal feelings towards Alexina Angus, which were at that stage ambivalent.

"I shall go and see this firm Grigson's tomorrow," Kemp finished. "There's always the chance Mr. O'Connell left an address with them. It might be a good idea for someone at your end to go and see this Sadie Brown."

"I think Grace might like to do that herself. It's not as if we're making a proper inquiry, and she can always say it's because of the family relationship. What's your feeling about this whole thing, Lennox?"

Kemp was undecided. "I'd like to hang on a bit longer up here. I just don't know. They've been married three months now, they must have settled somewhere... I'll stay a couple of days and I'll let you know if anything develops."

EIGHT

FIONA O'CONNELL looked at her face in the glass of her dressing-table and frowned, displeased at what she saw. Winter was never a good season with her; she took little exercise and was inclined to overeat, particularly creamy pastries of which she was fond, to the detriment of her figure and complexion. Not that she had ever held either in high regard, being disposed to ignore them as permanent disadvantages rather than seek their improvement. But now her attitude to such things was stealthily changing. Out of habit she continued to buy the ladies' magazines which had for so long been her mother's sole reading matter. She found herself scanning their glossy pages with an awakened interest, studying the articles on diets and beauty aids as if learning a new geography.

Fingering the silver-backed brushes that had been hers since girlhood, she remembered the weekly ritual of camomile flower shampoos and lemon rinses her mother had once insisted upon to keep the fairness in her daughter's hair. Alas, that hair had darkened to indeterminate mousiness by the time Fiona was into her teens, and even Anna Davison-Maclean had given up. "You'll never be a beauty, Fiona, you haven't the grace..." The heavy line of the girl's mouth had set stubbornly as she accepted the verdict.

With an air of distraction she now pulled out a tendril from the tight roll she wore behind her ears, and laid it along her cheek. She had already taken a tentative nervous step forward; she had bought and used an advertised rinse to lighten the colour. Terrified that it might give that brassy look which she associated with women not of her class, she had been sparing in its use—so much so in fact that it seemed to her own critical appraisal to have made very little difference. Next time, she vowed, she would make it stronger.

Yet, that morning Jeannie, the local girl they had taken on as a maid at Lochaline House had said to her: "You've nice hair, Mrs. O'Connell, you ought to have it done proper." Had it been said out of kindness, or pity? Fiona was unaccustomed to such personal remarks. Now, she wondered. Perhaps Jeannie was right. Fergus would be pleased, and really that was all that mattered.

As she thought of him Fiona dropped her eyes from the mirror, afraid of their giveaway expression. She loved him. The intensity of feeling she experienced when he came into her mind—and these days he was seldom absent from it—shook her to her bones, and her desire for him came in surges over which she had no control. It was as though her body no longer belonged to her but was given over to forces outside herself, yet at the same time she was acutely and disturbingly aware that by its responses, its stirrings and palpable sensations, it was beginning to enjoy a life of its own. The impulse that drove it, however, was something Fiona had failed so far to come to terms with; she had been ill prepared for the effect of such physical passion.

When she had entered upon the marriage she had done so coolly at first, looking at it from all sides, weighing the pros and cons—as she had put it to herself, not daring to voice such things to anyone else, not simply out of natural reticence but because she had no one—and finally deciding it was quite a sensible step to take. Fiona had always considered herself to be a sensible woman. "You haven't much in the way of looks or charm," her mother used to say, "but at least you've got sense, Fiona." As if sense was the last quality one could wish for in a daughter.

Well, where had that sense gone now? Fiona felt she could no longer look at things straight. The world—her world—had changed as if an earthquake had rocked the roots of her being and molten lava now flowed beneath the surface, distorting and recreating her inner landscape.

She turned to the bed and glanced down at the pillow where his head rested at night beside hers. Her eyes dilated under the pressure of emotion. Of course he was shallow, a foxy fellow, a trickster, and they had little in common—save in that bed. But he must be kind at heart, she tried to convince herself, and if his feelings did not match hers in depths surely that could be remedied? If only she were more attractive!

She went slowly downstairs past the great window above the loch, blue this morning and glinting silver in the pale February sun, and, with the sudden determination characteristic of her kind once a decision had been reached, entered the kitchen.

"I've been thinking about what you said, Jean. Perhaps I should have my hair done. I'm sure there must be a salon at the Hydro in Rothesay." When she had travelled with her mother there had always been a resident hairdresser in the hotels where they had stayed.

Jeannie looked doubtful.

"It's out of season, Mrs. O'Connell. I wouldn't think the salon would be open in the wintertime."

But having once made up her mind Fiona was not easily put off.

"Well, surely there must be somewhere else... Where do you go yourself?" For the girl's reddish mop of curls was certainly not naturally so.

"Oh, I've got a friend works at that Mrs. Ferguson's in Montague Street. Now there's a good hairdresser, Mrs. Lisa Ferguson. A lot of the ladies on the island go to her. She'd work wonders with your hair. Would you like me to ring for an appointment for you?"

"No, thank you, Jean. I shall see... I might just take the car into town this afternoon and have a look round. Mr. O'Connell's in Glasgow today so there's no need to prepare any lunch. I'll get my own, and you can go off at twelve."

Fergus had been going up to Glasgow quite frequently lately. Clearing up some business there, he would say to Fiona, or seeing some of the chaps.

She wondered helplessly at times if he regretted giving up his work. She could see that he wasn't used to leisure. Somehow she had always envisaged men as busy creatures, fully occupied in masculine pursuits

when not with their womenfolk. It had been so with
her father. When not actually in his office or travelling, he had chaired meetings, attended committees,
dined at his club or lunched at the Stock Exchange.
Even at home he worked on business papers, scrutinized the markets and engaged in long telephone discussions with his associates, while in his leisure time
there had been golf, shooting or sailing.

Fergus did none of these things. She had been surprised to find how unathletic he was; he knew nothing of sport save football on television, and the
occasional Saturday match when Rangers were playing at home. Was that what he'd said that morning?
That some of his pals might be going on to Ibrox? She
hadn't been listening. As for sailing—Fiona went to
the back door and looked wistfully out at the little
yacht riding at its moorings off their own private
jetty—he was keen enough to learn but she could tell
he'd never handled a boat in his life. Of that life she
knew little, though he was not slow in talking about it.
But it was too far removed from anything she had ever
known for her either to enter it in imagination or understand it.

He's of a different class. It might have been her
mother talking. Fiona shut the door firmly against the
cold wind and went upstairs again to put on her tweed
suit. She would go into Rothesay and see if this Mrs.
Ferguson's place would suit her.

After lunch she drove the three miles through the
pretty countryside—apart from the stupendous
mountains of Arran across the tongue of water, the
scenery of the island was not breathtaking—and

parked sedately in the Square behind the Castle. She had not been much in the town itself, only to visit the Estates Office to negotiate the purchase of Lochaline House which had taken her fancy the moment they saw it. "It's that water beside it," Fergus had teased her, "you're a great one for the water, Fiona." It was true. There were no other houses along the shores of the loch, only the upland farms looked down on it, so that it was almost a private lake, and that thought had excited her and led to her purchase of the small craft. She would sail on these waters, and indeed on the few calm days they had had since settling in early in January she had already done so, managing the sails and the rigging at first clumsily, then with more skill as she remembered her father's instructions that long-ago summer.

He had come down to Rothesay a lot in his sailing days, anchored in the Bay along with his fellow yachtsmen and had talked with enthusiasm about the town as one of his favourite places. But Fiona had been disappointed on coming to it. When the Navy had had its supply ships there in the busy war years there had been a bustling prosperity and sense of purpose; now it had a desolate abandoned air, the buildings fallen into disrepair, the inhabitants lazily accepting the worsened times. Perhaps when the summer comes, Fiona thought, it will be different.

Despite the sunshine this particular afternoon Montague Street was deserted. She found the salon without difficulty. It was called the Bijou Beauty Parlor, for reasons that were obvious since it was tiny, crushed between a butcher's shop and the Laggan

Arms, a dour-looking pub shuttered and silent, the victim of falling trade even in this town where the drinking rate was well above the average. The Bijou had once been painted a bright blue but the sea air had bleached the peeling paint and stripped the façade in places down to the bare wood. Over the door were the words: "Prop. Mrs. L. Ferguson, Beauty Counselor." Fiona gave it one quick glance as she passed. Was the spelling due to American influence, or a hint as to the status and education of the Prop.? The window held some dusty cosmetics, a tattered price-card and a few faded posters of eye-bright girls with many-hued tresses round their heads like Catherine wheels. Not my sort of place at all, thought Fiona, hurrying by. Perhaps she ought to wait and ask Fergus; he would be the right person to advise her about her hair. Yet she paused at the butcher's shop, and stood looking in at the chops and steaks neat in their white plastic trays scattered with imitation parsley. No, she would not ask Fergus; she would surprise him with a new modish hairstyle.

She walked slowly back, caught up in a sudden fresh image of herself. She reached for the shop door handle, and found it locked.

Dispirited, she turned away.

"Is it Mrs. Ferguson ye're lookin' for?" The butcher had come out to his shop-front and was watching her.

"It seems to be closed." Fiona made a helpless gesture.

The butcher consulted his watch. "Och, Lisa is maybe takin' a long lunch-hour. There's nae a lot of trade about. She'll be up the stair in her flat. Ye can go in that door there."

"Oh, I shouldn't want to intrude..." Fiona began, but the man had turned away as a customer went into his shop.

Fiona hesitated. Beside the salon door of the Bijou was another, even smaller, painted in the same blue, with a gold knob on a rickety lock. Fiona put her hand on the knob and pushed. She had a heavy, strong way with her, not exactly clumsy but not delicate either and the feeble lock gave under her touch. The door opened and she was faced with a steep flight of stairs.

Slightly appalled at the damage she had done to the door, Fiona went forward and upwards. I can only apologize, she thought fiercely. Having come this far, I might as well go on.

At the top of the stair there was a landing with three doors leading from it. Two were ajar revealing what were obviously kitchen and bathroom. From behind the third door came the murmur of voices.

Fiona raised her gloved hand and knocked gently but again her nervousness betrayed her and the impact was heavier than she realized. The door had not been properly closed and now swung wide before her so that even standing as she did on the threshold the whole room was open to her view.

It was an untidy apartment but bright as the sun shone in upon a scatter of chairs, a table with the residue of a meal upon it, and, taking up most of the remaining floor space, a huge double bed swathed in pink flounces. A coverlet spotted with cabbage roses had half-slipped to the ground, revealing two naked bodies entwined and on the rose-red pillows two heads, one dark, one fair, that even as she watched raised themselves and stared at her with dark holes for eyes.

Fiona gave an agonized shriek of recognition, cut short as she stuffed her fingers in her mouth and blundered out. Blindly, holding on to the walls on either side, she went down the stairs and into the street.

"Who in God's name was that?" Lisa Ferguson struggled up on her elbows as Fergus leapt out of the bed and began searching for his trousers, swearing like a navvy.

"My wife, that's who it was . . . My bloody prying bitch of a wife . . ." His hands were shaking as he tried to fasten his braces. "This'll take some explaining, Lisa my lass, 'deed it will. I'll have some fast talking to do before I can get her over this . . ."

Lisa watched him, tolerant amusement in her baby-blue eyes. How funny men are, she thought, as he hopped about putting his socks on. All this fuss just for a bit of sex. She could always see the comical side of things.

NINE

Of course there was an unholy row. If words were burning brands the walls of Lochaline House would have crackled and gone up in flames. Only Anna Davison-Maclean's repeated admonition ringing in the ears of her betrayed daughter—"Not before the servants—" kept the temperature down in the daytime. But for three nights the storm raged unrepressed until it spent itself and Fiona lay, whey-faced and silent, rigid as the tree-trunks outside the windows, drained of all feeling save a dumb despair. Incapable alike of comprehension and the will even to try, she at last let her body make its own mute surrender.

Fergus was used to women who made scenes and had ridden out many such encounters before but the intensity of Fiona's anger shocked him, and roused deeper sensations. Like an animal stirred in its lair and flexing sleepy claws, he too had been driven to darker thoughts within himself. Outwardly he practised all his seasoned cajolery and soft talk to coax her back into his ready arms. Given time—and the usual routine assurances expected as the aftermath to such scenes— she would come round as others had done in his past happy-go-lucky experience. Only the damned nearness of her money gave teeth and bite to his efforts this time. He must tread warily, and that small furry animal lurking in his mind closed its paws and waited.

Lisa Ferguson took it all philosophically as one used to the slings and arrows. A widow approaching forty, she went her own way with men, despite wagging tongues. So long as her business didn't suffer—and she'd found that people didn't necessarily expect their hairdressers to be overtly moral—she had her own independence. She was fond enough of Fergus but knew she'd shared his favours in the past with many another. She guessed he'd come back to her sooner or later.

When he did come climbing up her stairs bearing a clutch of beer bottles, she was ready for a laugh about the episode. To Lisa the spectacle of Mrs. O'Connell standing there looking at their naked bodies had by this time taken on an aspect of high comedy. She was quite prepared for her and Fergus to roll about in helpless merriment at the farcical situation—after their usual jolly love-making, of course. But she saw immediately that Fergus was not going to have it so. There was a grim look on his face that she had not seen before.

He threw himself into a chair, and poured out some beer.

"We have to talk seriously about this thing, Lisa. It'll have to be talked about . . ."

He didn't tell her all that had passed between himself and his wife; even in his present bitterness Fergus had some decent reservations. He did tell her, however, what had been the outcome. It had been inevitable.

"It's more than just jealousy." He got up and stalked about the apartment, running his fingers through his hair. "She's had a shock."

"Oh, come on now, Fergus. She must have known you had a life before she met you. She's no kid."

"I don't understand her half the time myself. But I have to stick to her—well, for the time being anyway, though she gives me the scunner... It's the bloody money. She'll give me anything but money..."

"Well, you married her for it." Lisa had no illusions. "You'll just have to hang on in there... What's she got to say about me?"

"We'll have to cool it for a while, Liz. I told her it was the last time anyway...that afternoon, you know. She only came in by chance..."

"That bloody lock, I should've had it fixed." Lisa wasn't really worried; she'd dealt with deceived wives before. And Fergus was no great shakes as a man. She looked at him now: there was sweat on his forehead and in his face the gnawing anxiety of a non-thinking male forced to consider things beyond his scope.

"I told her I wouldn't be seeing you again—that you were just someone I used to visit when I came to Rothesay on business trips..."

"And I lured you into my parlour, you poor old fly!" Lisa's laugh was wholehearted and generous.

"It's not funny." He glared at her.

"I can see it's not for you."

"All I need is time. She'll come round. But it would be better if you were away for a while."

"Well, that's easy enough. I was thinking of taking a wee holiday. There's no trade here until Easter."

Fergus looked at her eagerly. "You mean it, Liz?"

"Sure, why not? I can close down for a month and be off to Glasgow. I could do with some new clothes, and a bit of buying for the season."

His face cleared. He hadn't expected it to be this easy.

"I'll make it up to you, Lisa, really I will. She'll get over it, and then you and I'll be OK. It was mebbe a bit soon for her to find out, her not being a woman of the world like you." He made it sound like a compliment and Lisa took it as such.

"The odd thing is, you know," he went on, "she reminded me of you the first time I saw her. Not that she's got your looks, of course, nor your figure, but just something about the way she sat at the table in that hotel. Perhaps that's what made me pick her up."

"And then you found she'd the moneybags? You're a right scoundrel, Fergus." Lisa Ferguson patted her blonded waves complacently; she was proud of her creamy skin and trim waist. "Maybe you can wangle a day off and come and see me in Glasgow, eh?"

He glowered. "I'm no' goin' to be on a leash to any wife. I'll see you, Liz, never fear. But not here in Rothesay."

"Don't worry, Fergus, I can be packed up by the weekend and take the Sunday boat. If your Fiona comes nosing around here she'll see the shop's shut up and you can tell her I've gone."

He put his arm around her in sudden gratitude; Fergus always appreciated the easy way out of a dilemma—particularly if taken by someone else. As he felt Lisa's familiar warmth, breathed the spice of her scent, he tightened his hold.

"God, Lisa... I don't think I can do without you..."

In his mind he saw his sullen sulky dame sitting out at Lochaline House nursing her wrath, and a shudder went through him.

Lisa Ferguson pushed him away. "Off with you, Fergus O'Connell... else she'll be in at that door again!"

But he couldn't join in her laughter. His thoughts were in a turmoil, brooding on the injustice of it all. He'd like to drive Lisa up to Glasgow himself. Should he mention it? Too damn risky. There must be another way. It went against the grain in him to feel such frustration; in the past he'd had the sense to keep his aims within limits and not reach for the stars. Even his betting had been on a modest level—a canny realism saw to that. Now with a fortune so near his grasp he began to understand the big gamblers, the men who staked everything on one throw of the dice. New ideas teemed in his brain, thoughts he'd never had before, and all of them coming smack up against the wall of his wife's obstinate stinginess. What had she given him? Only a car—and she'd seen to it that she'd kept her own—and for that he'd given up his freedom! The rover in him chafed at the reins she held, his animal nature clawed at the bars she'd forged. He couldn't stand it much longer.

Lisa Ferguson was startled by his seriousness when he turned to her. It made him more attractive, and this time she didn't push him off.

TEN

By Saturday evening the Bijou Beauty Parlour was swept and tidied, a hanging card in the window intimating its closure until the end of March. Upstairs Lisa hummed happily to herself, planning tomorrow's departure. She was a person easily pleased by immediate prospects so long as they were concerned with her own private interests—and these were humble enough: a change of scene, and the chance to indulge pet pastimes.

She would go window-shopping, make the round of the department stores, picking dresses off the racks and trying them on; take light lunches and dainty teas high above Sauchiehall Street; go to a show or a cinema in the evenings; gossip with friends; put her feet up in comfort at some not too expensive hotel; have a couple of gin and tonics in the lounge, then bed and a lie-in in the mornings. Why not? She could afford it—and the fifty pounds Fergus had tucked into her blouse was an extra bonus. Ruefully he'd said it was all he could spare at the moment. That shrew of his kept a tight fist. But Lisa bore no malice. She was not one for thinking too far into the future and her sudden holiday held enough small delights ahead for her to forget all about Fergus and concentrate on herself.

She would wash and set her hair, have a nice leisurely bath, put out her nicest undies, her good travel costume—should she wear the cashmere or the Shetland sweater, or that new Viyella blouse? Cerise was a lovely colour; she would do her nails to match. You had to dress smart to go to Glasgow, people looked at you there... She was bored with Rothesay in the wintertime. The summer frocks would be in the shops by now.

Her thoughts ran on as she trotted about the flat, clearing the food from the fridge, cooking her supper, laying out her holiday wardrobe, polishing her best shoes. She'd buy some sandals, white strappy ones. She'd have her hair expertly styled in one of those posh places where they treated you like a lady. In her profession she knew all about the importance of personal appearance. She'd been letting herself go a bit lately—Rothesay in the off-season didn't demand much of a standard. It was high time she had a good bleach job done on her hair. Although naturally blonde, it tended to darken under winter skies and woolly caps. Why not have it done properly by other hands than her own? There were some stunning new tints on the market, from honey-gold to razzle-dazzle strawberry pink. She could take it; she'd always been a beautiful woman. And it would be good for her summer trade. Someone had told her about that foreign chap at that new health farm hotel on the outskirts of Glasgow who was a wizard with hair. Why not? She must look out that brochure she'd been given on the place. Might be worth a visit to get herself in trim for the season, and pick up a few professional secrets at the same time. She'd a bit of money put by and no one else to spend it on. Life wasn't so bad after all.

She put Fergus O'Connell and his dreary marital problems right out of her mind; she was off to enjoy herself in the bright lights of the City.

WHICH WAS ONE THING Lennox Kemp was certainly not doing that same Saturday evening as he leaned on the bridge over the Clyde and looked down at the oily waters of the Broomielaw. His visit yesterday to Grigson's had produced no address for the elusive Fergus O'Connell although it had served to expand a little his knowledge of the character he was seeking. None of the travellers had been in but the manager had talked freely enough.

"He was always the fly one, Fergus, but we could never fault him at his job. He got fat orders all right the years he was with us. Fallen off a bit lately—maybe he was getting past it. But then the trade's changing—not so much scope for his kind any more."

"I gather you found him reliable?" Kemp put it carefully. He had been frank about the reason for his call; that his interest lay in Mrs. O'Connell rather than her husband.

"I'll only say this, Mr. Kemp. I'd trust Fergus O'Connell with my cheque-book any day—but not with my wife nor any of my daughters. Surprised us to hear he'd got married. Of course he only lost his first wife back in the summer, but then I gather they'd lived apart for years anyway. But he never struck me as the marrying kind... Love 'em and leave 'em was his motto."

He looked at Kemp shrewdly.

"I'm told she's got money, this new wife. That would explain it. He just gave in his notice here and was off by the end of December. Said he'd let us have an address when they got settled. We've heard nothing since."

Disappointed, Kemp had last night telephoned his lack of success to George McCready, and hinted that the chilly city was beginning to get into his bones and he'd like to return South.

"Stay where you are till Monday," said McCready, "We took a run out to that place in Southend and hadn't any luck there either. Sadie Brown's away for a few days but a neighbour told Grace she's expected back Saturday afternoon so we'll have another try. Grace thinks that if this fellow O'Connell has a sister, then she'll know his address. God knows why she has such faith but it's all we've got to go on... I'll give you a ring tomorrow night."

So Kemp was left with time on his hands in a place he neither liked nor understood. A bitter wind was blowing hard up the river, and suddenly above the vapours of the City he got a whiff of salt air, the smell of the sea, a reminder that ships had once sailed right into the heart of Glasgow.

"Hae ye a match?"

It was a shambling old man who held out his ragged coat for shelter as Kemp lit his stump of cigarette. They both leaned on the parapet of the bridge.

"Aye, I mind when they quays doon there were a' busy. If it wisnae the trippers goin' doon the watter on the *Queen Mary*—that 'ud be oor ain steamer, ye ken,

not the big yin—it 'ud be the Irish boat sailin' on the
night tide, and many's the stormy crossin' I've had
once ye got beyond the Firth . . ."

"Seems like there's a gale coming up tonight," said
Kemp, turning up his coat collar and shivering.

"Aye, the hatches'll need to be weel battened doon
the night. Ye'll no' be a seafarin' man yersel' then?"

"Not likely." Kemp smiled. "I prefer to keep my
feet on dry land."

Yet, as the old fellow shuffled off, Kemp looked
once more down at the grey-brown river slapping at its
banks and was momentarily caught by that sense of
wonder and adventure which cannot help but be part
of the whole mystery of shipping; the putting out on
to dark unpredictable waters of any vessel, those impudent constructions of timber and steel, bearing their
microcosm of the urban world they synthesized; gal-
leys and cabins, decks and holds, bars and bottles.
What had Macgonagall said? "Oh wonderful city of
Glasgow, with your triple expansion engines . . ."

He grinned, feeling better. He pushed his way along
Argyle Street as the football crowds trooping out of
the station converged on the city streets, and the pubs
opened. It was a jostling, raucous, fairly good-
humoured and lively throng eagerly anticipating the
Saturday night ahead, loud with the local vernacular
which defeated him, but for all that, the sight and
sound of the people cheered his spirits. They think
they're second to none up here, he thought, and
maybe they're right.

His dinner was interrupted by a call from a jubilant
McCready.

"We've got the fellow's address. A postcard came for his sister. Wait now... it's Lochaline House near Rothesay in the Isle of Bute. You get down there right away..."

"Don't be daft." Kemp was succinct. "They don't send wee boats over there at night. Even I know that. It'll have to wait till the morning. How did the interview with Mrs. Sadie Brown go?"

"Oh, I left it to Grace...I don't think they hit it off exactly. Grace was a bit stuffy about it. Didn't think much of Sadie Brown as a sister-in-law for her niece. But no matter... We've got their address. Just you go and see them and make sure Fiona's all right, and that she writes to her aunt."

"Did you not try the telephone?"

"Grace has tried but it seems there's no number for that address. The postcard to the sister says they only moved there in January. Anyway, you're on the spot, Kemp. You could wrap the whole thing up in a day... And be back here on Monday."

McCready had reckoned without the minor accidents which bedevil even the most hopeful of projects, and the complexities of the Clyde sailing system in winter. Kemp's friendly receptionist had doubts about the plan.

"It's Sunday, mind. Even if you catch the eleven o'clock boat from Wemyss Bay you'd no' be there till near twelve with the wind that's blowing, and the only boat back is the one-thirty. It'd no' give you much time to visit folks on the island..."

And I have to find this Lochaline House, thought Kemp. Allow some time for that, and a good talk with Fiona... Enough anyway to reassure her aunt. He made up his mind quickly.

"Better have my account ready tomorrow before I leave. I'll not come back to Glasgow. I'll get the morning boat, stay one night in Rothesay and I'll motor straight South from Wemyss Bay on Monday."

"If your friends don't put you up then you'd best go to the Glengariff. It's the only decent place open there in the winter. At least for a gentleman like yourself, Mr. Kemp."

Kemp thanked her, glad to have made this impression, and retired to bed, once again to be a victim of the sound and fury of the gale shaking the window-frames like a demented orchestra as a storm blew up during the night.

It had not lessened by Sunday morning as he drove out of Glasgow seeking the coast road. He missed it twice, backtracked, cursing his own stupidity, and finally emerged between the green hills as the sun came out and shone golden on the Firth below him. But he was already late and a fallen tree at Inverkip delayed him for another frustrated half-hour. As he slid the car down through the rose-red sandstone cliffs and the neat snug houses of Wemyss Bay he saw the ferry leave, churning up milky-blue water at its stern as it was manoeuvred from the pier and set its course for the island.

There was nothing he could do except wait—yet again. He parked his car where it would be first on the one o'clock boat—though he doubted there would be much of a rush. Indeed, watching how the waves lashed the rocks, he wondered that anyone should trust either themselves or their vehicles to the squat unlovely craft now ploughing its stalwart bows into the troughs as it was caught mid-channel by the full force of the gale sweeping in from the south-west.

He went and bought a paper in the tidy glass-roofed station where hanging baskets of geraniums and trailing ivy were evidence of a happier clime. A pretty place in the summer days perhaps, but he sought the haven of a café and hot coffee.

Despite the wind tearing at the roots of his hair as he stood on the upper deck of the steamer which had—it seemed to him miraculously—weathered the crossing and returned by one o'clock for him and a handful of other passengers, he found the trip exhilarating. It was the same surprising sensation he had felt up on the Braid Hills that day in Edinburgh, and he wished, fleetingly, that Alexina Angus was beside him. This would be her natural place. Away to the west beyond that ring of mountains barred with snow, across that angry or that glimmering sea was where she had been born...

Descending the open stairway between decks he discovered the full meaning of the word bracing, and he threw himself gasping and breathless into the shelter of his car on the turntable. He drove gingerly down the ramp as the ferry finally came to grips successfully with the creaking timbers of the pier.

Rothesay didn't look awake but that might well be its normal winter appearance. He set off in the direction of the Glengariff Hotel which the receptionist had told him he couldn't miss. As the boat had sailed into the lee of the island and calmer water, he had seen the high façade rising above the houses lining the shore road, and had marked its name. He might as well go there first and check in, and also inquire how to get to Lochaline House.

ELEVEN

AN EXPENSIVE WARMTH sucked him through the revolving doors of the hotel into an atmosphere as discreet and comforting as a Swiss bank account. Once again Scotland was at her game of contrasts; up here the calm assurance of high-class prosperity, down below the seedy little town collapsing into picturesque ruin.

Yes, the suave young man behind the desk informed him, there could be a room for Mr. Kemp. From the quiet emptiness of the lounges glimpsed through glass doors there could well be a hundred. The young man twirled the register and Kemp signed, letting his eyes rove the sparse entries. A flamboyant scrawl intimated that Mr. and Mrs. L. Davison-Maclean had arrived yesterday. Kemp noted their room number. So, Lindsay had stolen a march on him. The trothless spouse would be Alexina.

"Lochaline House, sir? It's out on the West Road—only a few miles. Take the High Street, past the Castle, up the hill, and straight on. You'll see the loch from the road and the track turns off as you reach it. Will you be staying long, sir?"

"Just the one night." Fortunately for McCready's expenses, there were out of season rates.

His room looked over the bay towards Loch Striven; the hills skirting the water held colours riper and more robust than sky or sea, but Kemp didn't linger over the view. He found the West Road climbing out of the town and at its height saw the island spread before him, dwarfed by the Arran peaks. A sliver of gold among the brown moorland showed the little lochan, and on a spit of land running out into the water a tall grey house surrounded by a grove of trees. It looked lonely.

He braked as he came to the turning between the hawthorns, spindly and riven by the tearing wind. It was a bumpy ride over the potholes and through the muddy pools and he took it slowly. On the last bend he stopped and looked over the loch. The gale was blowing itself out but still whipping the water to storm-caps. On the far shore a yacht was beached, its hull at an angle, its mast drunkenly aslant. Near the jetty by the house an upturned dinghy tossed about like a matchbox on the glinting surface.

Kemp accelerated and edged his car round the curve of the roadway, then stopped again as he became aware of some kind of commotion ahead. There were cars and Land-Rovers; he saw the flashing light on a roof. Police. Men were running and he heard shouts as he got out and went cautiously forward.

"Sorry, sir, you can't go down there." A constable, polite, but barring his way.

"I was coming to visit Mr. and Mrs. O'Connell..."

"I see. Well, not just now, sir. There's been an accident."

"What accident? Can you tell me what's happened here? Could I talk to Mr. Fergus O'Connell?"

"I wouldn't advise it, sir." The policeman came nearer and lowered his voice. "That's his wife's body they've just fished out of the loch."

ABOUT AN HOUR LATER Kemp was knocking at Room 32 just along the corridor from his own. It also had a view over the empurpled hills but neither of the occupants were immersed in it. Alexina, after one startled glance at Kemp's face, turned away and set about clinking bottles and glasses nervously. Lindsay was sprawled in a chair, one elegant leg swinging, but his air of easy nonchalance was betrayed by his pallor, and his voice was shaking.

"So you got here too, Mr. Kemp. And I gather you know?"

Kemp looked at them both and said nothing.

He sat down on the edge of one of the twin beds and accepted a glass of whisky from Alexina's unsteady hand. She resumed her seat by the dressing-table where she ran her fingers through the short dark tufts of her hair, and stared at her reflection in the mirror. Kemp watched her curiously. She was drained of the colour that had made her vibrant, and her eyes were opaque.

"Well?" Lindsay demanded harshly, since Kemp made no move to speak, "have you seen the police?"

Kemp nodded and sipped his drink. The tenseness in the atmosphere was palpable. Alex dropped her head into her cupped hands.

"Out with it, man," said Lindsay. "What did they have to say to you? Have they taken that blackguard O'Connell into custody yet?"

Kemp could see that Davison-Maclean had been drinking; his pale eyes were bloodshot and his voice slurred.

Carefully Kemp put his glass down on the bedside table and took out a notebook. "I want to know three things," he said. "First, how did you know the O'Connells were here? Second, have you seen your cousin since you came to Rothesay? And third, if so, when?"

"Look here—you've no business questioning either of us like this." Lindsay's voice rose high. The veneer of the Edinburgh gentleman had cracked.

"I'm making it my business," said Kemp quietly.

Lindsay rose unsteadily to his feet and poured himself another drink.

"That won't help," observed Kemp. "I just want to find out where you stand—that's all."

"Oh, do stop acting-up, Lindsay." Alexina went over and sat on the floor beside him. She took his hand. "Can't you see Lennox is on our side?"

Lindsay gulped his drink. His eyes bulged with uncertain emotions he was struggling to contain.

"I've just heard that I've lost my cousin... It was a shock, I can tell you... Then you come barging in here with your questions when it's as plain as a pikestaff what happened!"

"That's as may be but I still want answers."

Lindsay slumped further into his chair. It was Alex who answered.

"The first is easy. Miss Maggie in Edinburgh, of course. The feu disposition of Lochaline House had to be put on the Register of Sasines—it's something like your English Land Registry. Anyway it was done through McLintock's and our Maggie saw the name Fiona O'Connell care of the Clydesdale Bank in Glasgow when the deed came into the office. She phoned Lindsay..."

"I see, and did you go out there?" Kemp saw the glance that passed between them.

"We scouted around yesterday afternoon," said Alex with some reluctance. "I know it sounds in frightfully bad taste now—in view of what's happened—but we did it just for a lark. We got a bit spiffed at lunch-time actually. Well, you've seen this place, the food's great and so's the wine..." She made it sound like the start of a naughty weekend—which perhaps it had been but her tone angered Kemp.

"This larking about... Did you in fact call at Lochaline House?"

"Stop badgering Alex." Lindsay pulled himself together. "It was my idea. I wanted to see what sort of place it was. No, we didn't call at the house itself. I'd no wish to meet this husband fellow. We drove around for a while, then we walked along the loch until the gale started up and it was too bloody cold to stay out there so we came back..."

"In fact you were just spying," Kemp remarked with some contempt. "Didn't you even try to see your cousin?"

"He did try, honestly. He tried to phone but there's no connection. Lindsay planned to visit properly this afternoon... Then we heard someone in the hotel talking about a drowning accident on Loch Aline..." Her voice sank and tears began to stream down her cheeks. "Oh, Lindsay love, if only we'd gone and seen her yesterday!"

Davison-Maclean put his arm round her shoulder. "Don't mourn, pet, you never knew her. And it wouldn't have made any difference. Fiona was doomed the moment she married that swine O'Connell."

Lindsay wasn't as drunk as he appeared to be.

"We didn't see anyone out there yesterday, Kemp, if that's all you want to know. I've only just got back from the police station. All they could tell me was that Fiona was dead, found drowned in the loch. An accident, they said. I soon put them right on that one. I told them all about Fergus O'Connell... He married my cousin for her money. Now she's gone and he did it. Oh, I told them the lot, but they wouldn't listen... 'Investigations will proceed, sir, don't you worry—'" Lindsay mimicked the Clydeside accent—"'if what you say is true it'll be for the Procurator Fiscal's office to decide...' The fools... Like as not they'll let O'Connell get away!"

Kemp had some sympathy for the sergeant. Lindsay Davison-Maclean's wild accusations might be well-founded—indeed Kemp himself was more than suspicious, and like her cousin he too was bitter that he had not reached Fiona sooner—but a police station in the immediate aftermath of a tragedy was no place in which to air them. He, with a more studied approach, had got further with the locals—not only the constabulary but also with those who had engaged in the futile rescue operation. He had mostly simply listened, finding the thrown comments between the men more interesting than any official statement was likely to be—at least for the time being. But Kemp had no intention of communicating any of this to his companions. He was not sure of either of them. Lindsay had an interest in the death; there was a fortune at stake and Kemp judged there would be few tears shed for Fiona from that quarter. Alexina had a softer heart, she had bewailed the might-have-been, but she was none the less Lindsay's girl; she would follow his line.

"Will you stay on here, you two?"

Again the swift look between them. Alex left Lindsay to answer.

He only shrugged his shoulders.

"No point. But by God I'll be in Greenock for the inquiry. That's under the office of the Procurator Fiscal here in Scotland—we don't have coroners. And I'll see O'Connell up in the Sheriff Court for murder before I'm through," he added viciously. "In the meantime I'm going straight back to Edinburgh to have a word with McLintock. He can't sidestep me this time—I'm next of kin."

Kemp eyed him speculatively. More than kin and less than kind . . . The will—or the lack of one—that would be the trend of Lindsay's thought.

"There is a husband," he observed mildly as he went to the door.

"Murdering bastard . . ." muttered Lindsay, but he got to his feet and held out a hand to Kemp. "We're in this thing together, you and I. It's for us to see that he doesn't get away with it."

But Kemp wasn't certain on either proposition. He preferred to take his own path, as he had always done, finding it the better way to discover truth and ultimately see justice done.

TWELVE

"No, Mr. Kemp." Inspector Duncan slammed the file of papers down on his desk with a thud, got up and stalked about the room, emphasizing his words with every firm step. "It's just not possible. There's no way yon Fergus O'Connell could have done it. Man, we've been over it time and time again..."

"I know," said Kemp wearily. "I've read all the statements. You've all been very cooperative, and I'm grateful."

He was tired. Tired of the granite-slabbed pavements, the incessant rain, the strait-laced churches, the dirty public buildings, the graffiti-scrawled hoardings where wit was sharper than hope, and the vast silent shipyards in this grey town of Greenock. He felt he was fast becoming a ghost haunting the Sheriff Court and the fiscal offices. He could not fault the authorities; they had gone dourly about their task. The pile of paperwork showed how assiduously they had questioned Fergus O'Connell, the hours of interrogation and the intense investigation that had gone into every aspect of the case.

Yet, in the end, the verdict had been accidental death and O'Connell had gone free.

"Your friend, Mr. Lindsay Davison-Maclean—now he'll never give up..."

"He's no friend of mine," said Kemp sourly.

"But the two of you are aye on the same old track. You're easier to deal with—I'll grant you that. He'll just not take no for an answer. You've a trained mind, Mr. Kemp, and you recognize police procedure. You saw that pathologist's report. Death by drowning, but death certainly occurring between eleven that Saturday night and ten the next morning... There was no shaking the medical evidence... And the Procurator Fiscal's department had done its homework. By God, they'd have got O'Connell for it if there was any way..."

"But he's got an unassailable alibi. I know. I know. I've even interviewed all those men myself."

Indeed he had. He had sat in many smoke-filled bars with them, talked to them for hours on end at Grigson's, drunk tea with them and their wives in suburban sitting-rooms, and found them all to be, according to their lights, honest citizens. The tale always tallied.

That Saturday night when the storm blew up and the little yacht slipped its moorings, Fergus O'Connell had been in Glasgow and under the eye of every man jack of them, from seven in the evening until early the next morning, attending a travellers' reunion, their annual booze-up and jolly get-together at the Grand Hotel. Each of them, separately and collectively, had told how they had supped in the same dining-room, drunk in the same lounge, swapped the same yarns, with O'Connell never out of their sight. Two of them had even shared his bedroom, had awakened bleary-eyed on the Sunday morning to watch him drive off on the road to Wemyss Bay to catch the first boat, the eleven o'clock, for Bute.

If only I'd caught that boat, thought Kemp savagely, I'd have seen O'Connell. Of course he wouldn't have known him then. Nor, for that matter, could he have saved Fiona. She'd last been seen by young Jeannie who had called at the House about seven on the Saturday evening with some eggs. According to the medical evidence, O'Connell's wife had probably drowned about the height of the storm, some time between eleven at night and the early hours of the morning—the body had been in the water nearly twelve hours before it was found.

Kemp went over the facts carefully in his own mind: the ferrymen at Rothesay had seen O'Connell drive off the boat just before midday that Sunday. His later statement to the police set out the bleak facts but what Kemp remembered was his own interview with the man when he was allowed to meet and talk to him, told him of Fiona's aunt and his own reason for being in Scotland. O'Connell was like a man in a daze, but his story held fast.

"I saw the yacht beached on the far side, and the wee boat drifting upside down near the jetty. And my wife was no' in the house. I shouted on her from room to room. Her oilskins were gone and those great boots she kept for the sailing when she'd a mind to it. Man, what was I but distracted? All I could think of was the loch . . . So I called the rescue services and the police. What more could I have done?"

It was true. The first indication that there had been a tragedy had come from Fergus O'Connell himself.

"Did you see the men take her from the water?" Kemp asked.

O'Connell shook his head. "They held me back. They had her taken straight to the hospital morgue. The police were all over the house. Oh, they kept their eye on me, all right. Wouldn't even let me have a dram, and by God, I needed one . . ."

Perfectly correct in their procedure though they had been, the local men, rescuers and police alike, had made no secret at the time that they suspected the husband.

"When did you see her, then?" Kemp inquired gently, although he knew.

O'Connell gave a shuddering sigh. "They took me into the morgue. Formal identification was what they called it—as if there was any need . . ." Then in a wondering tone, he continued: "She looked so peaceful. You can tell her auntie that . . . Despite the awful mess of her forehead—they told me the prow of the rowing-boat smashed down on it—she looked at peace. Her eyes were closed, she might have been asleep. I couldn't bear to look long at her. Mr. Kemp, it fair turned my stomach . . . God rest her soul . . ." He had crossed himself as though such a gesture might have been expected of him. Yet, though hesitant, it had not been entirely perfunctory, thought Kemp, remembering their interview. For all that O'Connell was shallow as tinplate, there had been about him a real air of stupefaction; he had behaved like one overtaken by a fate not of his choosing.

While the Inquiry was proceeding, Lennox Kemp had taken every opportunity to scrutinize all aspects of O'Connell's character, studying him like a bug under a microscope, but he still could not make up his mind about the man; he seemed to slip through the fingers like sand. There was no doubt that he was basically crafty, cunning, a devious and easy liar—in all a makeshift rogue, but was he a murderer? Certainly he had the stuff in him of which commonplace killers are made, given circumstances and sufficient inducement. He had wanted his wife dead, for all his feigned protestations that he had loved her; he had needed the money; there were rumours of rows. The background to the marriage had an awful banality about it; the pathetic spinster avid for romance, unsure in her new lone state, rich in everything except companionship, and the man seeing his chance, for him too an opportunity to ride out his middle years on a bed of roses... He was going to lead the life of Riley, his landlady had said... Something had gone wrong. Or, looked at from another angle, something had gone supremely right, for here was O'Connell now master of a fortune and rid of a wife who, from all accounts, had been something of an encumbrance.

Certainly the Procurator Fiscal, whose powers under Scots law correspond more nearly to a Continental investigating judge than to an English coroner, took very seriously the possibility of murder by the husband in the circumstances of the case; it was the Fiscal's duty to assemble all the evidence before recording a verdict, and if there had been the least doubt then a fatal accident inquiry would have been ordered. But for all Lindsay Davison-Maclean's wild accusations, and despite the suspicions of the police—who recognized as Kemp did the predatory nature of O'Connell—there was in the end no gainsaying the facts.

FACTS. What the prosecutor must have, hard and dry. What the lawyers must have to secure a conviction. Facts—they saved O'Connell.

For the other side of the tragedy was borne out by clear factual evidence. The time of death, the state of the poor body brought in from the loch, the disposition of the two boats. A farmer on the hill out with his dog about midnight to bring in a lambing ewe had seen the yacht adrift, caught in the gale scudding the surface of the water. So that's what Fiona had also seen. Her precious boat loose from its moorings. Had she thought she could save it? Had she taken the dinghy from beside the jetty and tried to row out to the yacht? A stupid enterprise, but people had spoken of her obsession with her new little sailing craft. It was possible. Anything is possible when you cannot unlock those hidden springs of action which motivate people even into the most hazardous of attempts. Yes, of course Fiona might have done just that, gone to her own destruction in a frenzied effort to rescue what had come to be a symbol of a fresh start in life. She had been clad for it. Her thickest tweed skirt, two heavy jumpers and her recently-purchased oilskin jacket— the things she wore on her few experiments with sailing on the loch. She knew little of wind and weather, she was inexperienced on the water, no matter that she loved it.

It could have happened that way. And that was the way it was taken, as a tragic death by misadventure.

Kemp felt that he had, once again, taken up too much of Inspector Duncan's time. But one point that had arisen still scratched in his mind.

"That will," he said stubbornly, "that's the thing I cannot understand."

"You mean our Scots law? That we still admit handwritten, unwitnessed testaments, not signed and witnessed by all those people in the presence of the testator and in the presence of each other..." Duncan gave a great hoot of laughter.

"Look at the trouble your English wills take—they need three sane people all present at the same time. In Scotland we only need the one—that's the beauty of the holograph writing. A document in the handwriting of and signed by the testator or a document attested as such," he quoted patiently, airing his knowledge which Kemp suspected had had recent refreshment.

"I'm not concerned with the niceties of your old Scots law," said Kemp somewhat testily, "it's just the timing of that particular will."

"I see." Inspector Duncan sat down again with a sigh. "Well, I have to admit it was one of the strongest pieces of evidence of motive we had against O'Connell. That she should have made it that day, that Saturday, in her own handwriting—and that's been proved—properly set out and dated—oh, she knew what she was doing all right."

"Leaving dear Fergus, beloved husband, all that she possessed."

"Aye, it sticks in the gullet. But I'd swear Fergus O'Connell was shattered when he saw it. We had him under our eye, ye ken, when we came on it in her desk and I've never seen a man so dumbfounded. He'd not expected it. I'd give my Bible oath on it. You've met him, Kemp. Yon's no' a man that's deep enough to hide himself. Not from the likes o' me. I've seen all sorts—mostly criminal. No, no, I'll take nae credit for it... But O'Connell, I know his sort and they canna fool me. When we showed him that will he was like a man possessed, no' like a man who'd inherited a fortune."

Kemp looked across the desk at Duncan and had to believe him. Yet the fact of the will rankled, as he was certain it must rankle with Lindsay Davison-Maclean. No wonder Lindsay was out for O'Connell's blood; if it were proved that O'Connell had murdered his wife, then he could not benefit from such unlawful act and Fiona's whole estate would pass to her cousin.

"And you've no doubt the will's genuine?"

"That's not for me to say, Mr. Kemp, but my colleague in Edinburgh has had a word with the late Mrs. O'Connell's lawyer and he let slip the word that the handwriting's hers all right... We had to contact Edinburgh because of the fuss yon cousin has raised—and he seems to have friends in high places—but it's my opinion, for what it's worth, that Mr. Lindsay Davison-Maclean will just have to lump it."

Kemp reflected on his own last meeting with Lindsay which had taken place, at Lindsay's request, in his Morningside flat. It had been amusing to Kemp to hear the Edinburgh law student inveigh wildly against the Scottish system which screened from unwelcome publicity anyone concerned in a fatal accidents inquiry. How Lindsay would have enjoyed seeing O'Connell pilloried in the Press when the story broke; how a crowd outside a Coroner's Court might have howled for his blood—a man who had so obviously married for money and in the eyes of such people, pub gossip being outside the sub judice rules, must somehow have contrived her death. Yet Kemp himself appreciated the fairness of the Scottish procedure which ensured that there would be no premature Press coverage likely to embarrass the defence should the inquiry lead eventually to a criminal trial. And in the case of Fiona O'Connell or Davison-Maclean—in Scotland she was still allowed either name—the Fiscal had been satisfied as to the cause of death, that she died by misadventure, and therefore no further inquiry had been ordered.

Coming down the stairs from Inspector Duncan's office with the man's final words in his ears, Kemp felt a sense of relief. Now he would leave this bleak Northern town where only the rain danced happily on the hard pavements, and only the wind whistled merrily round the corners of the old tenements. He didn't know which he hated most; the grey stone ''lands'' half-demolished or the jaunty new housing estates crawling up the green hills that had given the place its name.

His car was ready packed and pointing South, yet some perversity made him walk instead down to what only he as a stranger would call the waterfront.

Here where the two halves of the town were so abruptly divided, the east end with its derelict factories and idle shipyards and the west with its carefully planned tree-lined streets and squares of solid middle-class flats and villas, the dichotomy was clear for the eye to see. The Esplanade curved wide and grand, fronting the river as it opened out into the Firth, and across the water rose the hills, outliers of distant mountains, and that other mysterious Scotland of straths and glens, and far-off misty islands. If his heart well knew what had drawn him to this spot his rational mind spurned the notion as yet one more effect of this schizoid country on an otherwise equable temperament.

As he watched, a pale sun filtered through the clouds and lit the land beyond the Clyde. He had never understood before how mere beauty of scenery could bring such an ache, nor did he fully understand it now as he turned away.

But later, driving South to report the tragic outcome of the Davison-Maclean case, the thought of Alexina Angus clung to his mind and would not let go.

THIRTEEN

GRACE MCCREADY, as a good police officer's wife and thus accustomed to the premise that there is no such thing as abstract justice, took it well. She listened to her husband and Lennox Kemp arguing the matter out and saw that all had been done that could have been done. As a woman, however, and the aunt of the girl—as she still thought of her—she was naturally inclined to sorrow and after a time to contemplation of Fiona's state of mind at the moment of entering into the marriage, and thereafter. Kemp tried, as a man, to understand and, as an investigator, to satisfy this curiosity on her part.

"Fergus O'Connell," he told her, over scones and tea which made him think again of Alexina, "must have appealed to Fiona in some way. He's a good-looking man and used to charming the opposite sex. As to whether he's a nice man, well, I don't know... He's like shifting sands, there's no substance there... He was an honest employee of his firm—hard-working and dependable. I'm afraid his weakness was women."

Grace drew herself up as any respectable matron would.

"He seduced my niece. I thought so."

Kemp demurred. "I don't think so, Mrs. McCready. I think Fiona met him half way. I think each wanted something from the other..." He gestured helplessly.

"Do you think he drowned her, Lennox?"

Kemp bit into a scone, and considered the question.

"I think your niece was foolish to marry him. I think he also was foolish in that he took her for other than she was. Your sister—if I may say so—had brought Fiona up in a certain way... To value money and the things money brings." Kemp went carefully, for the ideas were his own and he was not sure how they would be received. "Fiona had been taught to hold on to what she had. I don't think Fergus O'Connell realized that fact when he married her."

Grace nodded, acknowledging the trait as a virtue.

"The Scottish instinct," she said with satisfaction. "What we have we hold, for we'd a hard time making it..."

"Something like that," said Kemp cautiously, "She didn't give him the run of the money he'd hoped for. To a man like O'Connell that could have been dangerous... But, no, I don't see how he could possibly have killed her."

"She would have been a good swimmer, Fiona. Her father taught her..." Grace McCready had not a strong imagination but she could not help what her mind's eye drew out from the discussions she had heard.

Kemp shook his head vigorously. "It would have been no good. That water was like ice, and the waves were high. That dinghy must have gone over like a cockleshell..."

"Her face was marked, the report said..." Grace would not let the scene go.

"Yes, I know. The pathologist was certain it happened when she was already in the water. It looked as though she tried to grab at the boat but a wave caught it and it smashed down on her head, and she went under... It was a wild night—no one could have lived in those waters."

Mrs. McCready sighed, and changed the subject.

"Were there other women in that man's life?" she asked, shrewd in her knowledge of the world.

"Of course there must have been but it would be a bit early in the marriage for anything like that to surface. Fergus would be too fly for that. There was some gossip in the town—that's Rothesay—about a hairdresser he'd been known to visit in the past, but nothing came of it. From what I could gather, she's a somewhat flighty widow with her own business, but there's nothing sinister about her, and folks say she never cared much for O'Connell anyway. I never did get to see her. She was away on holiday when it happened and her shop was closed."

"I wonder what took Fiona to Bute," mused Grace McCready inconsequentially. "I mind that my sister Anna hated the place. She said it was common—where the Glaswegians, as she called them, went for their holidays. Yet Jock went there a lot in his sailing days."

"Perhaps that's why your niece decided to settle there. It seems it was her decision to buy Lochaline House." Kemp had described the situation of the house to Grace: the grey stone building on the spit of land running out into the loch, the fir trees above it, the waters lapping at its garden walls.

"And it'll be all his now, this Fergus O'Connell?"

"I'm afraid so. Here are the photographs you let me have. She looks happy enough in this one." It was an old snapshot, two little girls of about twelve years of age holding on to the mast of a yacht, laughing, their faces upturned to the sun. "Who's the other child?"

"Let me see." Mrs. McCready put on her glasses and peered at the photograph. "Fiona's got on the striped jersey. I don't know who the other girl is. It must have been taken in Rothesay Bay—you can just see the harbour at the back there and the Bute Arms Hotel..."

"Which has since fallen down, I understand," said Kemp with a short laugh, "as the rest of the place seems to be doing. I only thought she must be a relative—there's a likeness."

Grace McCready frowned, and looked again at the snapshot. "Oh no, that couldn't be. There was only Fiona and her cousin Lindsay. It's probably just a playmate she had at the time. I see what you mean, though... That would be Jock Davison-Maclean's boat they'd be on." She made to put it away with the other photographs but Kemp reached out his hand.

"May I keep that one?"

"Because of the yacht?"

"I don't know. I'd just like to have it." Kemp put it in his pocket and took his leave, with a certain sadness. Memories of Fiona would live on here in Muswell Hill, not in the mansion in Bearsden given over to others, not beside Loch Aline of the cruel waves, but here in the heart of this stout ageing lady who would remember the pale girl and the unhappy life so tragically cut short. They would be memories tinged with regret but disciplined into an acceptance that, for some, circumstances can be manifestly unfair and must be contained as such. Some aspect of this regret suffused him as he said goodbye.

"I've let you down, Mrs. McCready." Not used to defeat in his line of business, he surprised himself by feeling the words deeply. "I think I should have done more." But she dismissed him with the resigned stoicism of the Scot by referring only to the surface of things.

"Och, never mind, Lennox. You did what you could. I only asked you to find her. What's done canna be undone..."

PART TWO

PART FIVE

FOURTEEN

It was in the middle of a cold May that Fergus O'Connell slunk back at last to Lochaline House. There was nowhere else for him to go. He had slipped over to Ballymena to some of his mother's people as soon as the funeral was over—a subdued ceremony in that same Bearsden graveyard where the previous October Anna Davison-Maclean had been laid to rest. The police had finished with him, he was told, and that was enough for Fergus. He was off like a scared rabbit to a place where they'd never heard of Fiona, and anyway had enough violent troubles of their own not to be interested in his. But eventually there was business to be done, and papers to be signed, and Fergus could no longer avoid the dreaded interview at McLintock's.

Because he dreaded it, and resented that dread, Fergus put on an aggressive attitude at odds with his usual trained salesmanship and presented to the tight-lipped Scottish lawyer possibly the worst outward aspects of his shifting character. Not that Josiah McLintock would have noticed, nor was he in any way astonished by the man in front of him: O'Connell was just what he had expected, no worse, no better. McLintock never had high hopes of his fellow human beings. In his profession he met them necessarily at a fairly low level; nervously expectant, suavely confi-

dent, or simply plain greedy. In O'Connell he per-
ceived all of these things and to hand over Fiona
Davison-Maclean's estate to such a one was suitably
unpleasant, but McLintock never shirked his duties
under the law; the will had been allowed to probate,
the documents had been drawn up, and so he watched
with calm legalistic impartiality as the shabby creature before him signed them, and came into his inher-
itance.

All the same, there was no small talk. McLintock
was brusque, icily correct, and there was no offer of
the usual client's cup of tea. Miss Margaret Muir
sniffed loudly as O'Connell passed through her office
on his way out, and she observed none of the usual
civilities.

"I'll no' go back there in a hurry," Fergus vowed as
he went down the steps into Frederick Street. He left
the stately purlieus of the New Town with a curse on
the whole bloody bowler-hatted brigade of them, and
sought a pub in Rose Street where he'd at least feel at
home. No need to worry, he assured himself, he had
the money now.

IF THE PEOPLE of Rothesay were surprised at his return to his house, with true Scots cunning they didn't
show it. It was: "Hallo there, Fergus, so ye're back
then?" in the bars, and a cheeky: "Will ye be wantin'
any eggs then, Mr. O'Connell?" from Jeannie when
she passed him on the lane. The truth was, though
they didn't like him, he was more one of themselves
than his wife had been. If there was a furtive quality
about Fergus now that he was back in Bute it was only

to be expected, and conversation with him was kept steadily to the weather, the times of the boat sailings, the state of the harbour and the price of drink. It hadn't escaped their notice that he was now a rich man, the owner of the fine estate and free enough with his money. He settled into Lochaline House like a hibernating animal, drawing its walls around him for camouflage, taking occasional forays into the town to make the rounds of the pubs but otherwise keeping to himself.

By the end of June, with the advent of a spell of good weather and the first of the summer visitors, Fergus O'Connell had become part of the scenery and the subject of, no less and no more, the normal gossip in a place inhibited by its narrow boundaries. If there were rumours that a woman had been seen about his place they were kept to a low key. Well, it was to be expected. He was that kind of man, wasn't he? Nobody blamed him.

Jeannie was working up at Kilmeny Farm, above the shores of Loch Aline, and she'd seen washing on the line at the House.

"They're no' his nighties!" she'd said with a laugh, "He's no' been long findin' a substitute!"

But if he had, she was not for showing off, for he never brought her into the town, and as entertaining at Lochaline House was out of the question, the Rothesay folk had to be content, for the time being, with rumours. That Lisa Ferguson's wee salon was up for sale hadn't escaped attention, and conclusions were eventually drawn.

"She'll likely no' want to show her face for a while," was the gist of the women's gossip, "Not that Lisa ever cared much for tittle-tattle—she's had ower much of that in her life already..." But it was to be expected that in these special circumstances a woman wouldn't want to draw eyes to the fact that she was setting up house with a man whom some still regarded as a murderer.

Soon Jeannie spread the word that it was indeed Lisa Ferguson's underwear that flapped insolently in the breeze beside the waters of Loch Aline.

"I saw her, plain's the nose on ma face—sunbathin' in a deckchair. She came over for the eggs right enough but she was that snooty... No like she used to be, aye ready for a bit talk. All hoity-toity, she's gone, like the high and mighty mistress of the house... Thank you kindly for the eggs, Jeannie, and good day to you..."

But the folks Jeannie told her tale to shook their heads sagely.

"Money changes people, and maybe Lisa's keepin' to hersel' for O'Connell's sake. Yon's a man, now, that doesn't want to stir things up. They'll likely want to live quiet."

Speculation as to whether he would marry her kept the bars and tea-shops busy until the summer season was upon the town and parochial matters were temporarily set aside in the bustle and preparation for the hoped-for influx of trippers. Fergus and his lady were left immured in their grey house by the loch, although it was noted that he no longer made his forays into the town bars.

"Lisa'll keep him well occupied, nae doubt..." Said with a knowing wink, and perhaps a touch of envy for O'Connell's choice, although when he did appear in Rothesay at the garages for petrol for his Mercedes or in the shops for stores, it was seen that it was uncalled for—he didn't look like a man to be much envied. He had grown grey and haggard, taciturn where he had once been matey, and he had a hunted look in his eye which warned off any who might have asked if he intended to settle down now with a new missus.

Only local lads who fished the loch, or boys from the farms who raced their mopeds down the rutted track, confirmed that O'Connell and Lisa were to be seen of an evening sitting on the low wall where the waters lapped or walking hand in hand about the garden. Mrs. Ferguson's staff—that is, the two apprentices she had employed—had been given good references to seek work elsewhere; they had no quarrel with that—jobs were easy to come by in the season—and the careful notice had included the explanation that Mrs. Ferguson was relinquishing her business interest upon retirement. It was an explanation accepted as adroitly as it was given, satisfying the civilized mores and to those who queried further, her local associates and former cronies, she gave out the impression that she was to become housekeeper to the owner of Lochaline House, a sad widower in need of such services. By such means, so long as the proprieties were, on the surface, observed, curiosity was at least allayed and the everyday world went on.

So the tragedy of the drowning and the unfortunate end to Fiona Davison's hopes of a new beginning to her life faded in the short memory, and the people of Bute, used to past dramas of drunks and drownings, and the perversity of fate, put the O'Connell case into the limbo of legend, and prepared instead to welcome the summer steamers and those intrepid Glaswegians who might still, out of either nostalgic yearning or present penury, think of their island as a holiday paradise. The others, they well knew, had long ago settled for Benidorm and the sun.

FIFTEEN

FROM THE WINDOW of his office Lennox Kemp had watched the greening of summer in the South. Even in Walthamstow the birds sang, and in the parks the trees put out celebratory leaves to catch their droppings. He sometimes thought albeit fleetingly of the bleak realities of Clydeside. Dark and true and tender, the poet had sung hopefully of the North. Kemp had not found it to be so. Give me the bright, fierce fickleness of the South—even the sun going down over Hackney Marshes—he said to himself, at least you know where you are; you trust in nobody, and nobody trusts you unless they pay for it. It seemed a better contract than in that other land where superficial values hid a darker, more secretive alliance.

July arrived, and the smoky evenings lengthened. On one such Kemp cooked himself a poached egg and was about to slip it on to a plate when his telephone rang. He considered letting it ring, then lifted the receiver.

"It's Alexina Angus. Remember me?"

"Of course. How could I forget? You are the taste of buttered scones to me. Where are you?"

"In Rothesay. At the Glengariff."

"With Lindsay, I suppose." Kemp's first lift of the heart settled down to normal. "Well, what can I do for you? Or are you just dialling the odd foreign number out of sheer boredom?''

He could almost see the pout of her red lips.

''I'm with Lindsay, yes. But, Lennox, I need your help.''

Kemp listened. He carried the phone over to his kitchen table, and started on his egg. She was a long time coming to the point.

''...so you see, he's losing his wits entirely. He's done no work for months. He simply won't let Fiona's case go...''

Kemp swallowed hurriedly. ''But that's all in the past.''

''Not for Lindsay. He's only just started.''

''I gather he's not in the room with you. Where is he?''

''He's up on the hill above Loch Aline—where he's been for the past two weeks. With binoculars...''

Kemp sighed.

''What do you expect me to do about it? If he's got the time and money to go bear-hunting, then that's his affair.''

''Lennox, you don't understand. He's like a man possessed. It's as if a demon's eating him. He's changed... You remember how easy in his ways he was—well, all that's gone. He has one idea in his head and one only. It's as if all the energy he never needed to use in the past has fused into one desperate channel. Nothing else matters to Lindsay now except to get Fergus O'Connell indicted for the murder of Fiona.''

It seemed that, far from accepting the official view of the death of his cousin, Lindsay Davison-Maclean had only just begun on his own personal vendetta against her husband.

Kemp was brusque.

"That's ridiculous, Alex. You know as well as I do that O'Connell couldn't have done it."

There was silence for a moment, then her small breathy voice came back. "Lindsay doesn't believe that. And now that Fergus O'Connell is back there at Lochaline House with that hairdresser woman as his mistress..."

"Tell me," was all that Kemp could say.

"O'Connell disappeared for a month or so, went over to Ireland they say, and the house was all shut up. Lindsay stayed in Edinburgh, chewing his fingernails. Then he heard O'Connell was back. Oh yes, Lindsay has his spies—even in Rothesay. So, here we both are..." She suddenly sounded very weary.

"Why me, Alexina?"

"Because I think you understand Lindsay. Because I think he might listen to you as to no one else."

Even across the distance he could feel the seductive force of her elusive personality. "He means that much to you?"

"We haven't anyone if we don't have friends..."

"Is that an old Gaelic saying or did you just make it up on the spur of the moment?"

"I thought you were a friend of ours." Again there was the suggestion of the pout.

"True—well, partly true." Lennox felt himself again slipping easily into her at times elliptical mode of speech. "Have you seen this woman of O'Connell's?"

"Only a glimpse. She's a flashy blonde—just his type. He hasn't married her yet, but there they both are sitting pretty at Lochaline House on all that money..."

"I can see you're as much affected as Lindsay," observed Kemp drily, "but it's O'Connell's money now and he can install a whole harem at Lochaline if he has a mind to. There's nothing you or Lindsay can do about it. It may seem to you that there's no justice but that's the way things are. Old Fergus gets the house, the money, the gold watch and everything..."

"It's not funny," the soft voice admonished him. "Why do you think I'm phoning you?"

"How the hell do I know?"

"Because I want you to come up here and talk to Lindsay."

"Oh no—not on your life..." Kemp's response was instant, and resolute.

"Please..." There was a desperate note in her plea. "I can't handle Lindsay any more. He's taken over a croft from one of the farms overlooking the loch. He watches the house day and night. He's like a stalker after the deer. And he's got a gun, Lennox..." Her voice dropped and there was the hint of a sob.

"He's out of his mind." But even as he said the words Kemp knew he would go up to Scotland. He had no choice. He distrusted this girl with the black eyes and the white forehead; he condemned her for clinging to her pseudo-aristocrat; he didn't understand her; but he wanted to see her again. He found himself saying weakly, "All right you've talked me into it. I'll come, if only to knock some sense into that laird of yours.'' He recalled, with horror, the prices at the Glengariff. ''I suppose they're on to the high summer rates at that classy hotel. I'll have to take out a mortgage on my flat...'' McCready wouldn't be paying this time.

It was a measure of Alexina's relief that she giggled before ringing off. She had said she would book him in, but he noticed there had been no offer to pay for his services—whatever these might be. As he sat back and looked at the phone he knew he was a fool to go. There was treachery in that Northern land, a treachery to which his heart was vulnerable.

At least I'll pack some sweaters. I don't trust even the month of July in Scotland.

SIXTEEN

KEMP NEED NOT have concerned himself about the weather. The waters of the Firth were in dulcet humour and smiled a benediction on the ferry as it chugged its way serenely across their flat blue calm towards the Island. The decks were crowded with holiday-makers, bright as the toytown flags strung from the mast and noisy as the wheeling seabirds. The band played *Scotland the Brave*, and down below in the bar the quick tills rang to sweeter music.

He drove off the pier, bemused, the sunlight in his eyes. The little town had come to life, its awakened shops gay with striped awnings and venturesome small tables askew on the pavements. The Esplanade gardens had grown almost vulgar under the strain of so much green lawn, and so many red geraniums, purple fuchsia and tight-packed yellow wallflowers. Copious spring rains and a few weeks of sudden summer warmth had brought forth jungle growth as rampant and outrageous as anything in the tropics. Men in deckchairs mopped shining red faces and rearranged their feet, while their wives let the knitting go idle and thankfully folded fat arms in pure content. People strolled purposefully about on the putting greens, sweating. No one was going to say it was too hot.

The Italianate gardens at the Glengariff were chaste and cool with their grey mossy stones and trickles of falling water. Yes, Mr. Kemp had a room, would he please sign in? He did, not looking at the price brochure discreetly turned the wrong way on the glass counter. What did it matter? He might as well be hanged for a sheep as a lamb, or whatever the phrase was, although that one sounded uncannily correct for Scotland, he thought as he followed the porter to the lift. No sign yet of Alexina although he had noted the L. Davison-Macleans, Mr. and Mrs., had the same room as on his previous visit, and they had already been there a week.

From the window of her room looking across the bay to the complacent hills above Loch Striven Alexina had watched his arrival. Why did I bring him here? she asked herself. He's not going to understand, and it'll only complicate things. Yet the sight of his thick-set figure, the square look of his shoulders, even the slightly comical aspect of the small bald patch on top of his head viewed thus from two storeys up made her smile. He can't do anything, she thought hopelessly with the inherent pessimism of her kind, yet I have to have someone. Lindsay is far gone into his own secretive world; he's slipping away from me . . .

Why did I ask the Englishman here? Will Lindsay even talk to him, will he tell him the things he won't tell me? But Lindsay liked Kemp. I've taken a fancy to him, he had said with exaggerated archness in that high affected tone, the precise upper-class accent he knew she hated.

She watched Kemp sling his bag out of the car, lock the door and walk towards the Hotel entrance. He's all of a piece, that's what it is; you could lean on a man

like that and feel safe. It would be like leaning on an
oak tree—

> *I leant my back unto an oak*
> *I thought it was a trusty tree,*
> *But first it bowed, and then it broke*
> *So did my true love tae me . . .*

She turned from the window, went over to the mirror and studied her face. What will he see? she wondered. Will he see clear through me? She drew a
delicate brown line along her eyelid and touched her
lips deep red. She arranged the bottles and glasses on
the table, and was ready for Kemp when he knocked.

He found her changed, then realized that it was only
her hairstyle, straight and spiky now rather than
curled, and worn low on her forehead so that it no
longer pulled at the white temples. Black-haired and
low-browed, she was, Pict rather than Celt, she came
of an older race and from a hidden people.

As they talked of this and that, renewing and en-
larging their acquaintance, he told her so. She gave
him the wide grin that was both monkeyish and beguiling, and raised her glass.

"They said it was the Spaniards wrecked from the
Armada."

"Don't you believe it. There's no foreign blood in
you, Alexina Angus. Your lot were building their
brochs and the black houses long before the invaders
came from Ireland or from Norway."

"What knowledge!" He didn't tell her he'd only
begun to study the history of the Islands since meet-

ing her. "Anyway, I was brought up in a single-end in
Glesca..." She put on her broadest accent. "Faither
was drowned at the fishin' an' ma mither made shawls
for the gentry till their wisnae ony money left and she
cam tae the City. It wis a lang way frae Coronsay, an'
there's nae romance in the road back frae the Isles."

"I never said there was. I'm not a romantic, and
neither's Lindsay. So what's all this nonsense of his
about O'Connell?"

She became serious. "It's not nonsense to him,
Lennox, it's become a matter of life and death. He's
sworn to get O'Connell for the murder of Fiona. He's
waiting for O'Connell to make one slip, give himself
away somehow, and when he does, then Lindsay wants
to be there..."

"Have you told him that I was coming?"

She shook her head. "I thought I'd take you out
there after lunch. You can say you're just on holiday
in Scotland and thought you'd visit Bute."

Kemp laughed. "You're priceless, Alex. Lindsay'll
never buy that. He knows what I think of Caledonia
stern and wild. You'd better tell him the truth."

"Right," she said, her eyes pert and knowing, "I'll
tell him the truth—that you came back to see me."

THEY DROVE OUT in the radiance of the afternoon sun
to Loch Aline sleeping golden between its watchful
hills. They stopped the car at the road-end to Kilmeny Farm and walked down the field to a cottage
crouched behind a hawthorn hedge. It was just a
bothy, nothing more, despite having been tarted up
with the trimmings of a modern bungalow—but red

corrugated roof, green shutters and a cute perspex porch couldn't hide its humble origin as a shelter for an ailing cow or a huddle of wet sheep. The farmer had seen the possibilities for a holiday letting, called it Wee Kilmeny and converted two tiny rooms into a box of a kitchen and a minuscule bedroom.

Alexina pushed the door open and called: "Lindsay?"

After the brightness outside the interior was dark as a hole and still held the yeasty smell of animals. Lindsay Davison-Maclean stepped down from the wide ledge under the window set deep in the old stone. He kept the binoculars in his hand as he came round the kitchen table and looked at them sardonically, but not without satisfaction.

"Well, well, look who you've brought . . . I wonder why? Never mind, welcome to my shooting lodge."

There were only two wooden chairs, a jug of milk and two mugs. Either Goldilocks wasn't expected or Baby Bear had been forgotten. Alex made coffee for herself and Kemp while their host poured whisky from a silver flask and drank from its cup. "There's a tumbler in the bedroom and another bottle in the larder." He made the offer with his usual courtesy, but Kemp shook his head. "Too early in the afternoon for me." He wanted all his wits about him this time round with Lindsay.

"Suit yourself. Now you're about to tell me you're only passing through during a tour of the Highlands. No—" as Alex was about to speak—"never explain. I'll take your presence here as a compliment."

"You needn't," said Alexina, flatly. "Lennox came to see me."

"And to revisit the scene of the crime, no doubt. Very wise, if I may say so, Lennox. You and I both have the same unfinished business on hand."

Now that his eyes had grown accustomed to the gloom, Kemp studied the other man. Lindsay wore a kilt in what Kemp took to be an appropriate hunting tartan. He supposed that in proper speech the definite article should be used—as though there was but one kilt for the whole of Scotland—but he had to admit that with his high-necked sweater and rough tweed jacket the garb of his ancestors (albeit landless Edinburgh gentry) suited Lindsay well enough. He looked lithe and workmanlike, no trace of the obsessed neurotic Alexina had led Kemp to expect.

"They're out on the terrace again this afternoon. Want to take a look?" He handed Kemp the binoculars and stood beside him as he knelt on the window-seat and levelled them.

The lenses were excellent and, with only a small adjustment, the distant scene sprang close in to Kemp's view. At the edge of a wood across the loch a roe deer stepped delicately from the undergrowth, raised a tentative head, then fell to browsing among the swaying grasses. Lower he caught the sparkle of waves where reeds met water, and, sweeping along to the right, he found the point of the spit, the jetty and the low stone wall surrounding the house. A break in that wall, a blur of colour, and he steadied the eyepiece.

He recognized Fergus O'Connell immediately. There he was sitting upright in a garden chair, a paper in his lap, his face turned up to the benevolent sky, as blameless-looking as those men in the Esplanade gardens. Kemp shifted the glasses slightly. The woman in the deckchair was brassy-blonde, her bare shoulders flushed pink between the straps of an orange sundress. She'll never get a proper tan under a Scots sun, thought Kemp irrelevantly, lowering the glasses.

"So there he is, sitting pretty with his lady-love," he remarked. "I don't know what on earth you can do about it . . ."

"That's what I keep on telling Lindsay." Alexina joined them at the window.

"There's many a slip," said Lindsay darkly, "I'll get the bastard yet."

He brought out an exercise book from a corner cupboard and slapped it down on the table. Kemp turned the pages. It was a neat and well-documented record of all Fergus O'Connell's movements during and after the tragedy on the loch. Most of the earlier material was familiar to Kemp from the file Inspector Duncan had let him see, and from his own investigation. After the case had been officially closed O'Connell had crossed to Ireland to stay with his mother's people in Ballymena; there he had lain low until the will had been admitted and upheld by the Scottish Court. He had then made several trips to Edinburgh to sign papers—information received and dutifully handed on to Lindsay by the invaluable Miss Muir. The elder McLintock had received him correctly but with scant ceremony, although his attitude had been somewhat mollified by O'Connell's apparent wish that the realization of the assets of his late wife should continue to be handled by the Edinburgh lawyers. O'Connell was proceeding with caution. When the house itself had been transferred into his own name, Fergus O'Connell had returned to it at the end of May. Two weeks ago he had been joined by Lisa Ferguson.

There followed a short dossier on that lady also. Lindsay had been busy. He had checked her on an extended shopping trip to Glasgow where she'd stayed at a modest hotel, and then to a health farm hotel on the outskirts of the City where she had apparently made a hit with the resident Italian hairdresser. Perhaps they had merely pooled their professional secrets. At any rate Signor Nerini's comment had been terse: "A nice lady, but common." Lindsay had sought opinions likewise in her native town of Rothesay where she was spoken of as a widow woman of some looks but little virtue. She had now sold her business in Montague Street and moved in with Fergus in what appeared to be a permanent arrangement.

"You've gone to a great deal of trouble," remarked Kemp, closing the book, "but there's nothing there that makes any difference to the Fiscal's verdict. Going back to that vital Saturday night, O'Connell was in Glasgow. Even if all his movements hadn't been accounted for by every one of his boozy chums, there was no boat back to the Island until the eleven o'clock from Wemyss Bay on the Sunday morning, and Fiona by then had been dead for hours. How'd you think he got across—by midget submarine or a helicopter? There isn't even an airfield. Who do you think O'Connell is—James Bond?"

Lindsay didn't even smile. With a curl of the lip at this puerile attempt at humour, he took the book and returned it to the cupboard. "He could have had an accomplice," he said, coming back to sit on the edge of the table, and Kemp realized he was serious. Lindsay's long fine nose quivered as if at the scent of quarry. An old portrait-painter would have lovingly highlighted its aristocratic bone structure and put a gloss on the pink and white complexion now faintly scattered with freckles. He'd look good in a powdered wig, thought Kemp, still irresistibly reminded of an eighteenth-century fop of the court.

Alexina shook her head vigorously. "That's just not possible, Lindsay. It was out of season. You know how dead Rothesay was—a stranger would have stuck out like a black man. The police told you all that . . ." She turned to Kemp with a helpless gesture. "He's been at the local station already with that wild theory—they only laugh at him."

"It needn't necessarily have been a stranger," said Lindsay stubbornly, and from the set of his mouth and the fanatical look which had come into the pale blue eyes Kemp began to understand what she had meant about obsession.

"You think this hairdresser woman was mixed up in it? I understand she wasn't even on the Island when Fiona drowned."

"Nobody checked that," said Lindsay quickly, "and of course she went to the local school with the sergeant, so she can't be accused of anything worse than going to bed with half the men in Rothesay."

"Your Puritan streak is showing," remarked Kemp sarcastically, then by way of drawing Lindsay's fire he added, "and talking of strangers on the Island that night in February, what were you and Alexina then—friendly aliens?"

It was the girl who made the startled movement. Her response was so swift and vehement that Kemp turned to her in surprise. He had only thrown in the remark as a diversion.

"But we were nowhere near Lochaline House that night!" She had leapt to her feet, her black eyes like coals suddenly alight. "What the hell are you getting at?"

"Cool it, kid." Lindsay put a hand on her arm and pulled her down, not over-gently. "You don't think our friend here meant it seriously? Look, you two, why don't you go back to the hotel? I'll come down for dinner later."

It was obvious that Lindsay wanted them gone; like most obsessions, his surveillance of the O'Connell residence was essentially a solitary occupation, and satisfied some need within himself. Kemp could guess what it was. Fiona's fortune had seemed to come close, then it had receded, but Lindsay still could not bear to let it out of his sights.

Kemp wasn't sorry to leave; the atmosphere in the tiny kitchen was stifling—and not only because of the animal smell. As they went out of the door he saw the shotgun leaning against the wall. The barrel shone as the sun caught its polished wood; its owner obviously kept it primed and ready. Kemp felt a twinge of unease as he tramped up the field to his car. Alex strode ahead of him, hands deep in the pockets of her black anorak. She didn't want to talk to him any more. He had offended her, and he wasn't sure how.

THE MORE GENIAL AMBIENCE of the Glengariff dining-room that evening in some measure brought the three of them together in something of the jocund spirit of their Edinburgh encounter. There was good food and wine, and they were surrounded by June visitors—holiday-makers perhaps too plebian a word—disporting themselves with the discreet sophistication of the bourgeoisie rather than with the unbuttoned licence of Clydeside hoi-polloi in the town below. Nevertheless, even here there was a carefree sense of relaxation as the chandeliers glowed amber on suntanned skin and into the clefts of white bosoms. Trays of lobster thermidor were no rosier than the abundance of warm flesh as the champagne corks popped and the talk grew higher.

Lindsay and Kemp could take pride in Alexina. She was theirs, and she was magnificent. In scarlet silk, her black hair screwed up in a spike on top of her narrow skull, a few strands falling Medusa-like across the low forehead, arched eyebrows pencilled thin and her cheeks precisely painted, she played both barbarian queen and barefoot peasant—Snow-White and Rose-Red rolled into one—with splendid effect.

"It's only make-up," whispered Lindsay. "She's just a dancing-girl from the Second City."

And dance she did. After dinner, in the ballroom when the couples began languourously to cover the floor, Alexina was in her element. Drawing attention, she never lacked for willing partners. The beat of the music, as even the members of the band quickened to something special, became more hectic; they sensed in the twirling red skirt and the tough little brown feet—she had soon kicked off her high-heeled shoes—an aficionado, a devotee of the dancing floor. Kemp found her like thistledown in his arms, thistledown and quicksilver. Relinquishing her to others was painful, so that as the evening wore on he sulked.

"She's mine, you know... Mine for life," said Lindsay in his most objectionable grandiose manner, sweeping her away.

Not by nature aggressive, Kemp at that moment could have hit him. That manner of Lindsay's towards the girl, his mocking but wholly confident assertion of some obscure right of ownership, aroused not only Kemp's quite understandable jealousy but outraged some latent sense he still held of chivalry.

When the party was over, the lights were dimmed in the vast empty rooms as the guests retired to connubial and other forms of bliss. Alexina kissed him on the top of his head—which was small consolation to Kemp as she turned away, Lindsay's arm firm across the red silk of her shoulders.

Kemp went solitary to bed, his natural inquisitiveness warring with baser elements he preferred not to think about. They were an ill-assorted pair, this scion of Edinburgh gentry and his dancing girl from the Second City, but it was not simple class which made them so—class was bridgeable if there was affection and he sensed little of that in Davison-Maclean's attitude. A deeper tie bound these two and roused

Kemp's curiosity. The girl was clever, sharper-tongued than Lindsay; like a small cat, she would scratch and bite if her interests were threatened. Why had she summoned Kemp to Scotland—was it just to protect these interests? The cause of friendship, she'd said. To hell with that, Kemp thought blackly before turning at last to sleep; it's not her friendship I want.

SEVENTEEN

KEMP'S MOOD had not improved by the morning. He took his breakfast in his room, ignoring the glory of hills and water beyond the window, and when Alexina rang he was curt.

"Lindsay's gone off up the hill..." she began. "I'm not interested in your Laird O' Cockpen," Kemp told her tersely, "I've got things of my own to do. Amuse yourself this morning—I'm sure you'll have no difficulty—some of your partners from last night will be glad to show you the swings and roundabouts..." He rang off before she had the chance to reply.

He had decided on the direct approach; he would make up his own mind instead of having other people's half-formed ideas and theories thrown at him.

He found Fergus O'Connell half-heartedly weeding the straggle of rose-bushes that grew at the front of Lochaline House. Here were few blossoms but their scent was sweet, vying with the honeysuckle rampaging along the wall. He straightened up at Kemp's approach and greeted him with little enthusiasm.

"Oh, it's you again. Kemp, isn't it? I thought all that was finished."

Lennox Kemp had a way with him, when he set his mind to it, of creating an atmosphere that disarmed hostility and he put these amiable tactics to good use.

"I'm on holiday on the Island," he explained easily. "I heard you were back and wondered if I could have a word. I've no quarrel with you, Mr. O'Connell, and indeed I'm sorry for the bad time you went through."

Mollified, the man grudgingly put down his hoe and sat himself down on the splintered wooden garden seat. Kemp perched gingerly on the other end, and offered him a cigarette.

"I've certainly no wish to stir up unpleasant memories," he said, "it's just that Mrs. McCready wondered if there was some little thing of your late wife's that she could have—a family trinket perhaps—I don't quite know how to put it—something to remember her niece by... It's a womanish kind of whim, you understand..."

O'Connell's jaw dropped, and he looked outraged. It was as if Kemp had asked for Fiona's teeth or a lock of her hair.

"Well, now isn't that the terrible thing..." His Irishness came into his mouth. "I've not taken the time yet to go through what she left, not at all. It'd be a distressful business." He lapsed into uneasy silence, his gaze going over Kemp's shoulder and roving the loch like a witless creature.

"Perhaps you might find something. There's no hurry. I'll be here for a few days."

"Will you now?" The news scarcely seemed welcome to O'Connell. Neither did the interruption that came from the porch where a woman had been watching them.

"It's near eleven, Fergus. Would you be wanting a cup of something? And your visitor, perhaps?"

O'Connell leapt to his feet as if stung. Kemp also rose and walked across the gravel to where she stood.

So this was the famous Lisa Ferguson. He was conscious of a certain disappointment, she was so exactly what he had been led to expect; there was no element of surprise. As she stepped from the shadowed doorway her pinkish-gold hair caught the sun, glistening like candy-floss. For all that it was early in the day her make-up had been proficiently applied—even if the feet thrust into white strappy sandals were not over-clean. She wore a cardigan over the orange sun-dress but it did not hide the line of her bosom, nor the trim waist. She was a handsome woman, and her demeanour showed she knew it.

O'Connell hurried between them. "Mrs. Ferguson's come to housekeep for me . . . A man can't manage on his own . . ." He stammered through the unnecessary explanation while the woman looked at Kemp with bright blue eyes, heavily ringed with mascara. "Mr. Kemp's just going, Lisa. Isn't that so, Mr. Kemp?"

Mr. Kemp had no intention of going even if the owner of Lochaline House, blocking the doorway with one hand on the jamb, was reluctant to give way to a stranger crossing his threshold.

His housekeeper, however, was moved by a more hospitable spirit.

"It's Mr. Kemp, is it? Would that be the one you told me about, Fergus—the gentleman who knew your wife's aunt in London? If you've come all the way from England, Mr. Kemp, we can surely offer you a cup of coffee.''

Despite the careful cosmetics, Lisa Ferguson had a second-hand, slightly shop-soiled look and the gay cotton dress showed dark circles of perspiration stain under the arms as she slipped off her cardigan and prepared to play lady of the house. Yet she had better manners than O'Connell, who had to step aside as she ushered Kemp through the bare panelled hall and into what was presumably the parlour.

It was a high-ceilinged room, pleasant enough although over-stuffed with dull expensive furniture—chosen and paid for by Fiona in the first flush of her marriage. As O'Connell subsided sulkily into an armchair Kemp felt a pang of sympathy for him; this was never the man's natural habitat. Commercial hotels and Mrs. Lambie's homely lodgings had been good enough for him in his happy-go-lucky travelling days. Was he perhaps regretting his translation to a higher level? He certainly looked ill at ease, even frightened, keeping his head well down and taking no part in the conversation. When he did raise his eyes Kemp caught a glimpse of panic in them.

But if the owner of the house was not entirely at home there the same couldn't be said of his mistress. She moved through the place as one used to all manner of dwellings, and set about producing admirable coffee with a smooth competence, bearing out Kemp's theory that women are on the whole far more adaptable than their menfolk. She also kept up a flow of inconsequential chatter as though Lochaline had never been the background to tragedy. Indeed, Kemp began to have difficulty in remembering that such had taken place—this deplorable Scottish habit of burying serious matters under the patter of couthie talk.

Mrs. Ferguson was an adept at it; after all, she had been a professional hairdresser, one who varied her speech to the requirements of her clients so that now she conversed with Kemp in a way that sounded natural to them both with, on her part, the shortened vowels and clipped consonants of the born Scot. Only when she addressed Fergus did she slip into the Rothesay vernacular, a mixture of common Clydeside and the gentler tone of the Islands.

Always intrigued by the way people spoke, Kemp listened to her with some amusement as she chatted to him about London which she had occasionally visited. "To do Oxford Street," she said, leaving aside any other attractions of the Metropolis.

"Have you always lived in Rothesay, Mrs. Ferguson?" he inquired pleasantly when he managed to get a word in.

"Born and bred here," she replied, "but for the time I had to go to Glasgow for my training."

"You come from a local family, then?"

"As anyone in the town will tell you," she replied, rather tartly. "Would you have another cup of coffee, Mr. Kemp?"

Kemp accepted, and turned to Fergus.

"I'm surprised in a way that you should have come back to live at Lochaline House, Mr. O'Connell." Kemp put what was more of a comment than a question, casually.

There was a trace of belligerence in the man's reply.

"And why should I not stay on here? It's my place—though there's some that say otherwise. Yon Lindsay fellow—have you seen him about?"

"Yes," said Kemp, "I've seen Davison-Maclean."

"He sounds a real trouble-maker, that one," said Mrs. Ferguson. "The things he's been saying about us! I'm a respectable widow, Mr. Kemp. Somebody had to come and do the housekeeping for poor Fergus—he couldn't be expected to manage on his own—but that Davison-Maclean fellow—he's been talking about me to people in the town. It's slander, that's what it is, nothing short of slander."

She sounded only mildly put out despite the strength of the words. She must be used to gossip, thought Kemp, if all they say about her is true. Here was surely a lady who was quite capable of looking out for herself. But money changes people, makes them more sensitive. It had certainly changed Fergus O'Connell from a smooth-talking salesman into a furtive hermit-like creature, only the occasional truculence showing the man he had been.

"You've not met Lindsay Davison-Maclean?" Kemp asked Mrs. Ferguson.

"I've no wish to." She bridled. "He's got no reason to wish us ill. All we want is to be left alone, isn't that so, Fergus?"

O'Connell squirmed deeper into his chair. "That's right," he muttered, "We just want a quiet life..."

"Well, I hope I shan't have to bother you again." Kemp rose and prepared to leave. "Oh, you won't forget what I came for, Mr. O'Connell? Some little memento for Mrs. McCready?"

Lisa Ferguson looked inquiringly at Kemp. O'Connell was floundering again. "Aye, I'll see what I can find ... Mr. Kemp has asked for something of Fiona's. For her aunt, you understand."

"It would be a kindness," said Kemp. "Perhaps you have a recent photograph of your late wife. Mrs. McCready only has some old family ones ..."

"That's the most terrible thing, now ... There wasn't the time ..." O'Connell stuttered.

The housekeeper's voice was soothing.

"I'm sure Fergus will find something to give you. He's never really sorted out his wife's belongings, Mr. Kemp. He's very sensitive about anything of hers. You can understand his feelings." She might have been discussing the frailties of a pet dog. "It does seem a shame that Fiona's aunt should have no proper remembrance of her niece."

O'Connell heaved himself up out of his chair. "Aye, I'll have a look ... You'll be at the Glengariff, I suppose? I'll maybe find something ... I'm not thinking straight about it all yet ..."

Straight thinking would not come easy to a man of O'Connell's shifty character but it seemed that his bodily comforts at least were being adequately taken care of by his new lady. She extended a gracious hand to Kemp upon his going, and it was Fergus who showed him out.

The porch, out of the sun, was chilly between its two grey stone pillars, and Kemp shivered. The door had been slammed hard behind him as Fergus scuttled back into the house like a rabbit into its burrow.

As he walked to his car, Kemp followed an irresistible impulse; he raised his arm in salute to the watcher on the hill. He saw a glint in the heather below Kilmeny, and hoped it was reflection from binoculars rather than the barrel of that primed shotgun.

Only one way to find out.

He drove the rutted road to the farm, then walked down the field past the cottage and on to the stretch of moorland, springy with exuberant heather. Lindsay had a spread rug in a windless hollow, a picnic hamper beside him and a bottle of whisky at his hand, the bracken-gold liquor glowing in the sun like the water of life itself. The gun rested nearby on a granite boulder, and in the shade beneath it lay a couple of dead rabbits, their furry ears already grotesquely stiff.

Kemp nodded towards them.

"I hope that's all you've shot at. I had a moment's worry down there."

"I saw you. Could have picked you off like one of these. The wife at Kilmeny will be pleased with them. Want some lunch?"

A cut of silvery salmon wrapped in watercress, buttered baps and cucumber, strawberries dipped in sugar, and a round of shortbread, it was a meal fit for a king. And kingly too was the setting, lark-song overhead, bees blundering about in the heather and the sun beating the daylight out of the loch below them. As if to give the food the respect properly due, neither spoke until it was finished, washed down by the benison of Scotch.

The silence between them was companionable, bereft of tension. Kemp wondered if his previous animosity towards Davison-Maclean had arisen solely because of Alexina. Without her presence they were simply two men who might possibly have liked each other, given common ground, wary perhaps as was their nature but conscious of the other's value measured on their own individual yardsticks.

When they did begin to talk, lying back on the softly yielding tussocks, the conversation was at first desultory and avoided all mention of the reason for their being at this particular spot. Lulled by the heavy scent of new heather and flowering gorse, Kemp felt himself responding to the man's charm—for charm he certainly had when he chose to put it out. It might have been superficial—like his adoption of the garb of old Gaul—a gesture to an audience, or evidence of his innate good breeding. With such courtly manners eighteenth-century noblemen had hurled insults at each other before reaching for their swords.

At last Kemp decided it was time he put his hand to the hilt. No sense in letting your opponent, no matter how hospitable, get his thrust in before you were ready.

"Pleasant though this shooting party has been, Lindsay, it's got to end. O'Connell and his woman are settled in down there snug as mice in a nest, and there's little you can do to disturb them."

"Snug they may be, mice they are not. Rats more like. I'm only biding my time. I'll rattle them, never fear."

"You'll need evidence."

"Perhaps that's just what I've got. The man's a rogue. I'll not let him get away with it."

"Presumably you mean Fiona's fortune? You'll never get him for her death. Is it the woman you're after?"

Lindsay gave him a hooded look, the milky blue eyes veiled.

"Aye, the woman. I've not met her yet, though I mean to have that pleasure soon . . ."

"And till then you'll spy on them—just as you did that Saturday when you spied on your cousin. Why didn't you go out then and visit her properly? Or did you go later in the night?" Kemp went on in the bland conversational tone they had both adopted and neither had changed even when more dangerous matters than abstract philosophy had been raised. They were like sparring partners amicably engaged, content to wait the chance of a telling jab to the jaw.

Davison-Maclean was repacking the hamper with the competent hand of one used to fending for himself.

"No, I did not. I was with Alex that night."

"So you say."

"And so will she say."

Kemp pondered the implication which came as no surprise to him. But he was roused.

"Why can't you leave her out of it? She ought to be back in Edinburgh getting on with her studies. She must have exams coming up."

Lindsay threw back his head with a great laugh which set the linnets flying.

"For an intelligent man, Lennox, you're a fool. Lexie doesn't give a tinker's curse for her studies. Why should she? She's got me."

"But she's got no future with you. You'll never marry her. For God's sake let the girl have her own life."

Lindsay flicked his finger at a spider busy mending his web slung between two spines of gorse. "You'll never understand. I am her life." The words were spoken with an arrogance just short of offensiveness. "Come on, give me a hand with the hamper, old son."

Speechless, Kemp took up the burden as Lindsay rolled the rug under one arm and shouldered the shotgun. They trailed back up the fields to the bothy as the sun began to sink in the smoky-purple clouds behind the hills of Kintyre, and the shadows lengthened. The last Kemp saw of Lindsay Davison-Maclean was the kilted figure standing in the doorway, his hand raised in an ironic farewell, the gun by his side, like a print from an old book of Scottish tales.

EIGHTEEN

BEFORE RETURNING to the hotel, Kemp went into the Rothesay police station. Sergeant McKelvie's smile of recognition was slow in coming and longer still to reach his eyes, which were wary. The two men had got on well enough when they had met previously during the February investigation, for McKelvie appreciated Kemp's logical approach to the matter, in marked contrast to Davison-Maclean's contemptuous dismissal of the local force in his excited campaign of hate against the dead woman's husband. And it was of Davison-Maclean that Kemp spoke now.

"Och, we ken he's back on the Island," said Mc-Kelvie, "and wi' a gun. He's ower early yet for the Twelfth, but of course he's got a licence for it—we checked that. He's a difficult customer—there's no tellin' whit he'll dae. We'll just need tae keep an eye on him, and he's been warned no' tae bother the folks out there at the loch—though why we should worry about the likes of O'Connell I dinna ken—we can dae without his kind in Bute. I never knew his wife, puir lady, but the man's a shifty character. I'm sorry he's come back."

Sergeant McKelvie had been on a course in Edinburgh the weekend of the tragedy and had only been hastily recalled to assist Inspector Duncan in the subsequent inquiry. As a result, he had borne the full brunt of Lindsay's wild accusations that they'd allow O'Connell to escape justice—accusations that ripened into diatribes against the police for incompetence. Though slow-spoken, McKelvie was not stupid; his interrogation of O'Connell had been vigorous, and severe to the point of harshness.

"I hold no brief for Fergus O'Connell," said Kemp, "but Davison-Maclean has a dangerous bee buzzing in his bonnet—and there's the lady to consider..."

"And who might that be?" Kemp had noticed that the Islanders spoke the proper English when they had the inclination; it often meant they wished to gain time.

"The housekeeper—Mrs. Ferguson."

McKelvie settled back in his chair. He had dark-blue Celtic eyes—put in with a sooty finger, the saying goes—that were impossible to read.

"Lisa Ferguson is well able to look out for herself. Mind you, I canna say I like her being out there wi' O'Connell, but she's her own way to make. I've known Lisa all my life—we were at the schule thegither."

"Has she got no family?"

"She's got nobody now. Her mother died a while back, and there wis nae father, ye ken. Lost at the sea... At least this wis the story. Her mother would have had a hard time of it, but Lisa grew up a real good-lookin' lass, and it wisnae lang before she was courtin'. A soldier he was frae one of the camps, Corporal Ferguson, and they got married whilst she wis still in her teens. But he was sent off to Korea and he got killed there... So Lisa would get a bit pension, and she went and trained at the hairdressing. Showed a lot of spunk, but that's Lisa. There's aye been some money about—mebbe she got it frae her mother, there's no tellin'... Anyway she set up her own business and that wee saloon o' hers has aye been popular. Pity she's sold it but mebbe she needed the capital..."

"She seems to be a well-liked lady." Kemp could put it in no gentler terms.

The sergeant cocked a knowing eyebrow.

"Och, there's nae harm in Lisa Ferguson, whatever's said by the auld pussycats in the town. If she's kept a warm bed for some, she's got the warm heart to go wi' it. I'm only sorry tae see her shacked up wi' yon O'Connell, but that's her business. She's known him long enough tae ken the sort he is."

Kemp grinned, to show that he also was a man of the world.

"And there's always the money now. It must make a difference. She might see herself as the mistress of Lochaline House rather than O'Connell's. Have you spoken to her since she's been back?"

"I have not. Few folk in the town have. Maybe for once Lisa's a wee bit ashamed... It's no' a nice situation to be in, is it now? They'd have been better tae have waited a while."

Having made a tentative opening, Kemp probed deeper at the risk of losing the friendly atmosphere.

"Do you think they waited *before* Mrs. O'Connell's somewhat timely death?"

The circumlocutory language he had deliberately used took nearly a whole minute to sink in.

"Whit d'ye mean by that?" McKelvie growled.

"I only wondered if this affair was going on . . ."

"Ye're no' to be sayin' things like that! And don't you be calling it an affair." McKelvie was angry now. "O'Connell's the sort that has a lot o' women. He's made nae secret o' it. He an' Lisa were in the same trade—they were auld friends . . . But it wis nae whit ye're suggestin' . . ."

"I was only suggesting that Mrs. Ferguson might not have been pleased at O'Connell marrying," said Kemp mildly.

"No! That wis never the way o' it. Lisa bore him nae grudge. She didna care for him that much, truth tae tell . . ." The sergeant stopped, conscious that he might seem to know too intimately what were the lady's preferences. "Well," he went on slowly, "that's what I heard, anyway . . ."

From her own mouth, surmised Kemp; she'd had a warm bed for the sergeant too in her time.

"I gather she was on holiday when the accident happened?"

McKelvie frowned. "Whit of that? She'd naethin' to dae wi' Mrs. O'Connell's death, and as far as the police are concerned, the matter's ower and done with. Ye're barkin' up the wrang tree, Mr. Kemp—ye're as bad as yon Davison-Maclean wi' his wild ideas."

"Far from it," Kemp assured him. "I'm only asking these questions to counter his allegations—and if necessary to protect Mrs. Ferguson from their effect."

The big policeman stopped glowering and calmed down. He took refuge in official language, abandoning his homely accent as if to put the conversation on a proper footing.

"We did scrutinize her movements that weekend," he said stiffly, "just as we did with other associates of O'Connell's when we started to check his story. Mrs. Ferguson was away up to Glasgow on a buying trip. She'd told everyone she'd be shutting up the shop for maybe a month or longer. The butcher next door saw her on the Saturday evening when she took down some food she'd left over, and she said she'd be leaving on the early Sunday boat. The men at the quay saw her go aboard—that's one thing about Lisa Ferguson, she's gey well-known. She had a bit joke wi' Lachie—he's the butcher—told him she was off to a health farm tae recover from the Rothesay winter..."

"And I suppose that was checked?"

"Man, d'ye think I'm blate?" The dark blue eyes glared. Then, seeing Kemp's look of total incomprehension, McKelvie guffawed. "Och, you poor English! I only asked if you thought me stupid. Of course we checked. As a matter of fact it wisnae difficult. There's no' many of these newfangled health hotels near Glasgow. It was me did the phoning, and I got on to her right away. She was at a place near Strathaven—had been there several days by then. I spoke to her myself. Of course I had tae tell her the reason for my call, without letting on we suspected O'Connell—it was too early for that. She was a bit shocked to hear about the wife's death but she said she never knew her and she'd not seen Fergus for a week or two... He was in the habit of calling in at her wee shop for a cup of tea when he was in Rothesay, for auld

times' sake—and that wis all there wis between them.
Oh, there's aye folk keen to make a bit scandal where
Lisa Ferguson's concerned but I can tell ye this, Mr.
Kemp—she wis never that much taken up with
O'Connell..."

And I'll just have to take your word for that,
thought Kemp, since you and she were old school-
mates and likely enough bedmates too when you were
a young man, you wily Scot.

They parted on amicable terms, however, but not
before the sergeant had a final word:

"And you tell yon wee Edinburgh lairdie tae pack
up and get out of his hidey-hole! I'll hae no madman
wi' a shotgun runnin' wild in my Island!"

"I'll do my best to persuade him to leave," said
Kemp, without much hope of success.

But wasn't that just what Alexina Angus had
dragged him up to Bute for? To knock some sense into
Lindsay, wean him from this foolhardy enterprise and
cure him of his obsession before it deepened into disaster. Yet all he, Kemp, had done so far was to see for
himself the effect of such obsession and—despite a few
sensible reservations—succumb to the same capri-
cious folly he'd been called upon to cast out? There
was something else Alexina had said: that Lindsay's
unused talents had fused into an implacable will bent
on—what? Not simply the acquisition of the fortune
which had escaped him, but a more sinister aim. If
Lindsay couldn't pin anything on O'Connell himself,
he'd bypass him and go for the lady—even if she were
as innocent as officialdom had found. But wasn't
Kemp being led by the nose down that same path?

Why otherwise should he be now strolling into Montague Street to have a look at the Bijou Beauty Parlour?

Its end of the street seemed to have fallen into a sad disuse. The shops opposite were boarded up, their leases presumably run out and, in such a time of recession, unlikely to attract new business, reflecting the little town's general air of slow decay. The Bijou itself was in the throes of a face-lift. "Under new management" said the notice stuck among the ladders and paint-pots but even this was not going to raise the derelict appearance of its surrounding properties. The pub to one side was shuttered—even the short summer season had not enlivened its lost trade—and on the other, although the butcher's was brightly lit, even its upstairs windows were uncurtained and blocked up. People didn't live above their work any more; Lachie would have a nice villa along the shore. At night the narrow street would be deserted, like an alley between warehouses in any city. Lisa Ferguson would have the place to herself after dark—a snug enough spot for a love-nest.

And far cosier than Lochaline House, for all its grand rooms and high gables. It was not to be wondered at that Fergus O'Connell had crept back here for more than cups of tea with his bonny blonde mistress, leaving his new wife out there by the cold loch. But what did that prove? He hadn't been here on that fateful Saturday night, and from all accounts Lisa Ferguson had gaily packing up her shop in preparation for a holiday jaunt.

From which she was now returned, refurbished no doubt and certainly resplendent, to sit in Fiona's house and hold O'Connell's hand against all comers. We just want a quiet life, Fergus had said on a plaintive note. And who could blame the man?

But out there on the hill stalked vengeance—in a kilt.

Lindsay had merely remarked, in his offhand way, that he intended to settle in at the bothy for an all-night watch. Kemp doubted that; Lindsay would be roaming the moors like a Border collie—Kinmont Willie on the trail of his enemies. He had some ploy in his mind, Kemp was sure of it, and he would brook no interference. It was going to be uncomfortable news to take back to Alexina.

NINETEEN

DINNER THAT EVENING was not a success. Alexina was on edge without the consoling presence of Lindsay, and Kemp too preoccupied with the possible mischief behind that absence. He could not even bring himself to tell her of the lunch in the heather—it seemed like a betrayal though he was not sure of what. All he said was that Lindsay would not be joining them, at which she merely looked grim and asked for more wine. Kemp guessed she'd already been well entertained in the cocktail lounge before he arrived.

"I don't know what Lindsay's up to," she said petulantly, jabbing at the fish on her plate, "and anyway, where the hell have you been all day?"

"Out and about. When did Lindsay first get the notion that Lisa Ferguson had something to do with Fiona's death? Was it before or after he'd heard she'd gone to live with O'Connell?"

Alex extracted fishbones from between her little white teeth. "Ugh...this sole said it had been filleted. How am I supposed to answer your questions? I know less than you do. All I can tell you is that he got some family papers out of McLintock's about a month or so ago. That bitch Maggie helped him— she'd steal the Honours of Scotland for Lindsay, that one." She bit back further opinion on Miss Muir, sensing Kemp's impatience. "Then he got word from

Rothesay that Mrs. Ferguson was out at the house with O'Connell, and it seemed to send him haywire... But he wouldn't say more, just that we'd come to Bute and he'd soon see they got their comeuppance.''

"Didn't he tell you why?"

"You've seen him, Lennox. He's grown as secretive as a squirrel with nuts, and that's what worries me. He's always let me share in his fun before this... Now he's closing me out of his life—and that's something I can't bear."

"Perhaps you'd be better off without him, Alex."

She frowned, and her black eyes dulled as if a light behind them had been dowsed.

"That's quite impossible."

Kemp had come to the same impasse with Lindsay, the same finality, as of an unbreakable code.

He sighed. "Well, it's your funeral." He at once regretted the banality as much as the tastelessness of the phrase but knew that further words on the subject would be as unprofitable. "Tell me one thing, though. That night in February, that Saturday night when you and Lindsay were here at this hotel, did he go out again?"

The waiter was at their table with the sweet trolley; she took a long time to choose.

Eventually Kemp said gently: "I asked you something, Alex."

"You're always on about that night," she said with a flare of impatience. "I've already told you. It was a wild weekend we were having, and I don't just mean the weather. We had a lot to drink..."

"You were drunk." Kemp put it brutally.

"We both were. But he didn't go out." She leant across the table and looked upwards into his face. "Lindsay did not go out that night. Does that satisfy your prying detective mind?"

Kemp gave up. "Well, he's out tonight, your sharp-shooter friend, up there on the hill," he said lamely.

"He'll come back in his own good time. Listen, Mr. English Investigator, I brought you here thinking you could help Lindsay—and all you've done is freak out with some nasty suspicious idea of your own. Or have you some other motive? Do you think you can split us up, Lindsay and me?"

It was too near to the truth for Kemp. It impinged on an inner discontent, an emotion not yet properly assimilated of which he didn't care, at this moment, to think. He decided to fall back on reason, the last resort and often the only one available.

"Don't you see, I need to know the whole of Lindsay's part in all this? I can understand him so far and no further. All right, he wants Fiona's fortune, he's always wanted it. He knew it would come to him in the end, and he was content to wait—until she went and got married. That shook him out of his lethargy. He followed her here in February. For what purpose? One only. To see her. To persuade her not to let the Davison-Maclean estate go to a stranger. So, he would take the first opportunity to talk to her... And I think he did..."

"No," she said stubbornly, "he didn't leave the hotel that night."

Kemp went on as if she hadn't spoken, ignoring the nervous stabbing at the ash-tray as she butchered another butt in the debris.

"I think that's why she made that will. In a fit of temper after she'd seen your dear Lindsay and heard his derision of the man she'd married. Oh, Lindsay wouldn't bother to keep that tone out of his voice, he's incapable of that kind of dissembling. But he'd never understand the effect it would have on her—he's quite insensitive to other people's reactions to that high-handed manner of his. You should know all about that..."

She shot a glance at him which had much of the Glasgow child in it. He'd struck the truth there, and there had been an answering spark.

He continued, feeling his way through the logic of his thought.

"Was there a blistering row between the cousins, or simply a cold reception? From what I've learned about Fiona Davison-Maclean, she wouldn't show her feelings—particularly to Lindsay; she knew he would only laugh at her behind her back. But she would take her revenge in the only way she knew—by making that will. I didn't know her so I can only guess at why she did it—possibly in a fury of resentment against Cousin Lindsay, whom she didn't like anyway and would like even less if he had sneered at her marriage... No wonder O'Connell was surprised when the will was found, and if he hadn't had that alibi he'd have been set up for her murder... Perhaps that was the whole idea. I'm only thinking aloud, Alex. You don't have to listen if you don't want to."

Alexina was carefully spooning brown sugar into her coffee as if counting the grains, not looking at him. There were little pinched lines round her mouth, and she was soberer than she had been earlier.

"I bet Fiona didn't tell Lindsay that O'Connell was in Glasgow—perhaps she wasn't sure herself. Lindsay probably thought Fergus was on a binge in Rothesay or in bed with a woman of the town. Lindsay takes a fairly restricted view of the lower orders. Did Fiona threaten she would make sure he never came into her fortune by making a will leaving it all to her husband? If his cousin really sent him off with that particular flea in his ear, Lindsay wouldn't go far. He'd skulk about—perhaps hoping the husband would return rolling drunk and he could be in on an enjoyable scene of marital disharmony. Then the storm blew up and the yacht went adrift . . . and Fiona ran out on to the jetty. . ."

Kemp paused, then went on in a quieter, more urgent tone.

"Look, Alex . . . I have to know . . ."

He spoke as one would to an infant who might take sudden fright and run away. "I have to know whether Lindsay did go out that night, and if he did, what time he got back."

But when, at last, she looked at him her eyes were without expression, dark and turbid as peatwater; she had withdrawn into that secret place she shared only with Lindsay.

"I have told you. Lindsay was with me here at this hotel that whole Saturday night. He never saw Fiona, and no one will make me say otherwise." She rose swiftly from the table with her usual economy of movement. "Ask when he gets back, and he'll tell you the same. I'm sick and tired of you. I'm going to bed."

He watched her slight figure thread its way through the diners. The resolute poise of her black head with its impudent top-knot, speared tonight with a silver dagger, tugged at his heart.

She'd go to the stake for him, he thought gloomily, and ordered another large brandy, not in any celebratory sense but rather out of a need for consolation even on a small scale.

The extra brandy didn't help, and he spent a restless night. When his bedside telephone rang and he struggled up to look at his watch, it was five o'clock.

"Is that Mr. Lennox Kemp?"

He recognized the voice.

"Yes. Sergeant McKelvie?"

"There's been a fatality." The man's voice was slow, heavy as the tread of his boots. "Out near Lochaline House. And you being a friend of his we thought you ought to know... Maybe you could help us break the news to the lady. They tell me she's at the hotel there... Mrs. Lindsay Davison-Maclean."

Kemp closed his eyes. Jesus, he breathed.

"Are you telling me it's Lindsay who's dead?"

"I'm afraid so, Mr. Kemp. We'd the word tae go out there, there was a shot heard by the folk at Kilmeny Farm. The body's been found down by the Loch. Mr. Davison-Maclean wis blasted by his ain shotgun."

TWENTY

THERE IS ONLY one way to live through a disaster and that is step by step, looking neither to right nor left, picking at the debris as you go, lifting the broken beams inch by inch, closing your nostrils to the choking dust, like firemen in a bombed building, alert for the moans of the living, respectfully realistic about the bones of the dead, and all the time wary of the one false move which can bring the whole toppling structure down around their ears.

The first shock, a personal hurt initially numbing, Kemp came to terms with as he dressed—he would not think about Lindsay now, those memories would come later. By the time he knocked on Alexina's door his mind was clear, his words already prepared. This could be no interval for compassion, pity or love, these would come in their course as the surges in his bowels told him only too well.

No more of that, he said to himself fiercely as he waited.

"It's me, Lennox."

She opened the door, he walked past her and closed it.

"Sit down, Alex. I have something terrible to say."

She sat on the edge of the bed. Her eyes were bright, sudden colour flushing her cheeks.

"There has been an accident, my dear. I'm afraid that Lindsay is dead."

She made no movement; it was as if the words had turned her to stone.

"I have to take you with me. Sergeant McKelvie phoned. He asked me to break the news to you... They have taken the body to the hospital but they need identification. I can do it, Alex... but I cannot leave you alone..."

Her silence was worse than tears. It seemed an interminable time before she spoke.

"How?"

Kemp told her the little he knew, no speculation, no imitation of hindsight, but the barest of facts.

"I'll come. Wait for me. No—not here. In your room."

Give her time and space to take it in, give her a respite to cry...

But when she came, dressed in her black trousers and anorak, her hair pushed up under a velvet cap, there were no signs of tears on the white face, a porcelain face blue-veined at the temples, her lips drained of colour to an ashen pink.

The drive to the hospital up on the High Road was short, and little was said, but the unspoken words lay between them, snarling the void like barbed wire. Dead now was all that innocence of anger or surprise which had added zest to their relationship. They were both entering a different phase, and they knew it.

Sergeant McKelvie and his men had been curious about Lindsay's girl; she was one who could not help but leave her mark. She had been with him in February, and here she was again, but although they called her Mrs. Davison-Maclean and the gossiping staff from the Glengariff had vouched for the registration, none of them imagined she was married to him. They treated her gently, and she answered their questions with composure.

"I'm his friend," she said, looking McKelvie straight in the eye, when she gave her name Alexina Angus, and her address the Edinburgh flat.

The sergeant drew Kemp aside.

"She seems a sensible lass... I'd no' ask her tae identify him if there was much disfigurement but it's just on the one side of his head... Will she be all right?"

Kemp nodded.

"We've got the body in the mortuary. It's this way."

Kemp went in with them. As the sheet was drawn back Alex gave a quick shudder, then nodded briefly and turned away.

Back in the hospital reception room she was given a cup of tea, and asked for a cigarette. McKelvie told them what had happened.

The police station had received a telephone call at eleven o'clock from the farmer's wife at Kilmeny Farm. She'd been shutting up the barn when she heard the shot. She and her husband, Peter Gallachan, discussed it, and came to the conclusion that it was a bit late for anyone to be out duck-shooting at the loch, and anyway there was only one person in their vicinity with a gun who would likely take to the hill at that time of night, and that was their visitor at Wee Kilmeny. Out of some sense of responsibility for him they went down to the bothy, and found him gone. Galla-chan confessed himself uneasy; he'd not believed that Davison-Maclean had rented the place just to do rough-shooting and, in his canny way, he'd been ob-serving the man's behaviour. He sent his wife back to the farm to phone the police while he set off down the road in the direction of Lochaline House. Asked why, he said he didn't know—he just feared for the folk there.

Sergeant McKelvie and a constable had arrived at the farm about twenty minutes later, and began a search of the surrounding fields. Just after midnight the dead man had been found behind a low stone wall which separated the scrub from the loch shore. No time had been wasted in getting the local medical practitioner on to the scene, and a hastily-rigged tent with a lamp set up.

"We were gey lucky there," said McKelvie, "Our local man, Dr. Pryde, had a friend stayin'—a foren-sic man frae the Scottish Office. It wis a busman's holiday for him. Anyway, the two o' them made a fair job o' it, a guid examination o' the body and the ground where it was lyin'—aye, and the position o' yon gun. It took them an hour or two and only when they'd finished would they let us move the body tae the mortuary here at the hospital. They want tae get started on the post-mortem as early as possible—that's why I phoned you... They're no' supposed tae start till there's been positive identification."

"It's Lindsay all right," said Kemp sadly. The red-dish-fair hair on the one side had scarcely been stained. He had looked surprisingly at peace, the lordly nose sharp as a knife-blade under the harsh ceiling light. Lost was his devilment now; Lindsay Davison-Maclean had gone to join those eighteenth-century ancestors whose manners he had so joyfully aped.

Kemp shook himself free from such fancies, and questioned the sergeant with more assiduity than McKelvie would tolerate. He held up a warning finger.

"Now, now, sir. Ye're going too far. It's no' for me tae draw conclusions. I canna speak till the medical men—aye and the Fiscal—have done their job. You should know that. Best ye take Miss Angus away now back tae the Glengariff. Ye'll maybe be wanted at the station later on in the morning. We've the inspector frae Greenock comin' on the first boat—then the inquiries can properly be set going. It's been a lang night and we can a' dae wi' a rest . . ."

Rest was the last thing on Kemp's mind, already awash with troubled speculation, the disparate pieces of the Fiona O'Connell case bobbing about like so much driftwood. His was not a nature to let things go when that kind of tide was flowing; when his instinct scented immediacy, as it did now, he must go with it, spurred by the realization that he had so far spectacularly failed to make the right connections. There were answers he must have, and only Alexina could give them. There were revelations to be made—even to be endured—before the truth was out.

He looked at her as they entered the silent hotel and she looked back at him with stark, frightened eyes. The night porter came out of his cubbyhole and approached them, obsequious and inquisitive, yet not unfriendly.

"I heard there'd been a tragedy, sir. Would the lady like some coffee? I've a kettle on the boil, and maybe you could both do with a wee dram?"

It seemed, in Kemp's experience, to be Scotland's answer in every woeful event, but he accepted the tray the man prepared, and acknowledged the kindness behind the thought even though prompted by curiosity.

"If you'd mind taking it up the stairs yourself, sir. It's not half past six yet and I'd not want to bother the kitchen staff. Thank you, sir."

"It's all right, Lennox," said Alex, as they went up together, "there's nothing improper. He thinks you're my English uncle come to keep an eye on me."

She was at least speaking again in her old manner, but she drew back and shook her head at her own door.

"Not in there. Your room."

No, she wouldn't be able to bear the sight of the double bed, Lindsay's splendid luggage, his gold travelling clock, the ebony-backed brushes, and his peacock silk dressing-gown still hanging on the wardrobe.

She drank coffee with greedy appreciation, the whisky sparingly.

"It'll soon be morning, Alex, don't you want to rest?"

"There's no rest now for either of us, Lennox Kemp. You and I know that."

"All right. We have to talk. I have to ask you again things I asked you before." Kemp ran his fingers through his hair, rubbed his forehead as if to erase the cobwebs self-spun within his brain. "But—first, did you hear all that Sergeant McKelvie said?"

"I wasn't really listening. All I could think of was Lindsay..."

"You see, it looks like an accident. That seems to be the conclusion the good sergeant is coming to—though he won't say, of course. That Lindsay went out with his gun in the dark, and as he was getting over that wall he slipped and the gun went off..."

Alex was chewing at her fingernails. She shook her head vigorously.

"That couldn't have happened—not to Lindsay. He's been shooting since he was a boy, bringing down ducks in thick mist, out for snipe on the marshes in less than daylight. He was trained in the game, Lennox, by men who knew the dangers. Besides, he was meticulous with his guns—he'd never make such a childish error as to leave the safety-catch off when climbing a wall..."

Kemp couldn't help but agree. "Even if he'd been drinking?"

She gave a bleak little laugh.

"The drinking went hand in hand with the shooting. The wee flask in the hip pocket and the gun—they went together. But the care he'd take with carrying that gun, why it'd be like the care of a mother with a baby!"

Kemp nodded.

"That's my thinking too. And Lindsay was a Scot—a turf-covered stone wall would be child's play to him even on a moonless night. He was sure-footed. He wouldn't be likely to slip. But what's the alternative? That he meant to do it? That shot was fired very close, Alex, from what I could see, and from what I heard from the police... If it had been from a distance it would have blown his head off."

He had deliberately tried to shock her, but her reaction was not what he had expected.

Her eyes blazed with anger. Well, it was better than flat despair.

"Of course he didn't! Lindsay would no more take his own life than I would. We were one in that, Lindsay and I... We had a bond of honour—neither of us would desert the other...!"

Kemp frowned. The words she was using were as if taken out of context, they were bookish, unnatural, and yet spoken with a ferocious sincerity. Here was the area he feared, the depths to which he had no plumbline, the puzzle of the bonding of these two: the rich Edinburgh grandee with his high-flown airs, and this modern waif of the Isles, her spunky wisdom hard-learned in the Glasgow streets. A romantic tale by that Scottish novelist—what was her name?—that Grace McCready had spoken of. But Kemp knew it had been no love-story. It wasn't love that had bound them, and Alexina was no grieving widow, though grief she showed in full.

As separate individuals she and Lindsay had stood out from the common clay, but they'd never have sold as a matching pair to ornament a household.

Looking at her perched uncomfortably on the edge of the bed, staring at nothing, a cigarette in the oddly exaggerated spread of fingers she adopted—and which at this moment must be out of habit rather than affection—Kemp was struck by her outlandish quality as he had been on their first meeting. Yet he knew her no better now.

"Tell me about yourself and Lindsay," he said gently, curbing his impatience to get to the nub of the matter.

She rose and went to the window, drew the curtains back and looked out at the pale line in the east where the dawn was stealing the darkness from the sky.

"He'll never see the sun rise," she whispered to herself, careless whether she was overheard. "Nevermore the heather nor the bracken at his knees..." Her shoulders moved as a sob forced its way into her throat.

"...A chief without a castle or a clan," Kemp murmured, the line springing unbidden from a corner of his desultory reading.

She turned on him then.

"What right have you got?" Her sudden incomprehensible anger blazed out as though he'd trodden on her foot.

"It's only a bit of poetry, Alex. When words fail we use other people's... It just came into my head. And it's not inappropriate."

"If I needed a coronach for Lindsay I'd write it myself. As it is, I hate all that Gaelic gallimaufry. My God, there was keening enough when his father died as would frighten off the herring gulls!" But she did come back and sit down, composing herself more neatly this time as if she knew where his questions were going, and was resigned to them.

"You've known Lindsay that long?"

"As well as the peasants ever know the gentry. The Davison-Macleans owned a piece of our island— bought it with their jute money, I suppose—and they'd be there in the summers for us to gaup at, with their fancy clothes, and their fishing and shooting, and their parties for the deserving tenantry. Took the place of the auld lairds who'd been gone long since . . . well, that would be the way they'd see themselves. A kind word here, and there maybe a wee job on the policies, a bit of sewing for my lady up at the Big House, and a pat on the head for the fisherman's child. D'you no' see how it was?"

Kemp shook his head.

"Like as not you don't. You've no modern notion of peasants—you English. And peasants, that's what the islanders became when the clan system was broken. The old family unity was smashed for ever so the poor folk were quick enough to huddle under the protective custody of the new lairds with their money, and their bloody paternalism . . ."

Her sociology studies had obviously taken her far, but there were layers below that Kemp felt he was only now starting to uncover.

She was quick to apprehend the beginning of his understanding.

"Of course I remember the son of the house, the young Lindsay Davison-Maclean. When my mother went up there to sew cushions, or take orders for the shawls that bleared her eyes all the winter, she'd take me with her to play in the gardens—be respectful and keep my thieving hands off the flowers—I'd see him. He was like a god, a golden-haired prince. I was well into fairy stories by then and he coloured my dreams. Something worse, something deeper I could never free myself from." Her voice grew tired. "Those long summers of a child—I'd be, I suppose, between five and eight—they went into my blood...and so did Lindsay...like a benevolent poison."

Kemp waited.

She took another cigarette before she spoke. "Like all lovely things, it ended. Abruptly. Mr. Davison-Maclean died and the estate was sold up. That same year my father was drowned, and my mother came to Glasgow to get such a living as she could. No more feet in the brown burn for me, it was guid hard Glasgow pavements from then on..."

A loss of paradise at eight years old. Kemp saw the way it had been.

"I met Lindsay again two years ago in Edinburgh at one of the University clubs. The hold was as strong as ever, and he just pulled me in like a monkey on a lead. I can't explain it further." She gave a short laugh. "The sentimental myth of Scotland—the land o' the leal."

"There's nothing wrong with loyalty. You perhaps took it too far, Alex."

"It wasn't love, you know... Not what you're thinking." She gave him a sidelong glance.

"I knew that. What puzzled me was why you lied for him. Because you did lie, didn't you, about that February night?"

She was chewing her nails again, and didn't answer.

Kemp felt himself growing angry. Time was passing, and there were things he had to do. Out of his frustration he spoke harshly.

"Damn you and your schizophrenic country! You're like the Spaniards, proud and servile, hard as nails and soft at heart as bad onions...!" He got up and stalked about the room, trying to push back the walls as if affected by an innate claustrophobia born of incomprehension.

"What was Lindsay after all? Just a moneyed fool aping some phoney historic power—based on what? Jute? Don't make me laugh!"

"You liked him," she said stubbornly. But his words had gone home as he intended they should, right back to put a hole through that childhood illusion. He wondered if this was how a psychiatrist might feel who has engineered a breakdown and has his client-victim just where he wants him.

"Of course I liked him." Kemp thought fleetingly of the lunch in the heather; Lindsay had woven his own spell there too. "And I might have saved him. Why didn't he tell me what he planned? Why did he think he was so clever? He didn't live in the real world either—he'd never been prepared for it... And that's why he's dead... Because he thought he could go it alone, solve the mystery of his cousin's death, find her murderer—and of course take back into his lily-white hands the family fortune. Face up to it, Alexina my sweet, it was the money that mattered to Lindsay, that was the only tradition he recognized—the tradition of his robber ancestors: if they were robbed, they went out and robbed in their turn. That's why he was out to get Fergus..."

"It wasn't Fergus he was after... Not lately, anyway..."

"Come on, Alex, tell me. It can't hurt Lindsay now. Tell me the whole of it."

She was crying, softly and hopelessly. Kemp looked at the broad white of her forehead under the tumbled black hair, the small straight nose and the trembling curve of her lips. He realized, with a shock not devoid of horror, that he was in love with her.

The sun was up, and the hotel already stirring. He went, unsteadily, to the phone and ordered breakfast.

TWENTY-ONE

KEEP YOUR FEET in that real world you're always going on about, said Kemp sternly to himself as he cleared the last of the bacon from his plate. He didn't want to think of that blinding revelation which had come upon him an hour or so ago; it was a blow to his self-sufficiency and would only bear scrutiny at a saner moment.

He had let Alexina eat in peace—or rather she had scrunched tiny pieces of toast laced with butter, refusing other food on the ground that she was incapable of swallowing. Despite this assertion of disability, he noted that she ate hungrily at the bread, and consumed cup after cup of coffee, heavily sugared. Content then that she would suffer no weakness from lack of sustenance, and having allowed her room enough in which to recover during the small intricacies of cups and saucers and the passing of the salt, Kemp also gave himself leeway, a breathing space. They both used the green marbled bathroom; Kemp showered thankfully, and shaved, pulling faces at himself in the mirror as he drew his sleeve across it—Alexina had steamed the whole place up with her scented bathwater.

The interim served them well, releasing tensions and, if not entirely dispelling mistrust, at least creating a climate for amicable dialogue, as such terms are used in international peace talks—and possibly meaning as little.

"Now, Alex, can we continue where we left off?"

Slowly and reluctantly, as if giving up a part of her past, she told him about that Saturday in February.

Lindsay and she had come out from lunch in high alcoholic bliss and driven around the Island until at last they stopped on the road above Loch Aline. "So, there's the O'Connell stronghold," said Lindsay gaily, leaping out of the car, "where Fiona, fair, fat and forty, hides away her low-born swain!"

Laughing, Alex had followed him down the rutted track, but pulled him back as they reached the house wall.

"We can hardly go calling in the state we're in, it would shock the douce, decent body that Fiona sounds to be from all you've told me."

They'd sheered off then, at the waterside, and run along the shore.

"Hand in hand, along the strand, we raced across the pebbles," said Alexina, her sloe-black eyes lit by the memory, "'Fee—fee—fee Fiona,' Lindsay hooted into the rising wind, 'come out, come out, where-ever you are! Come out, sweet coz...'"

They'd stumbled into the reeds, sending the wading birds squawking around them. "These damned shoes—I've lost a heel," Alex had wailed, and Lindsay had looked down at them with disdain. "Why do you wear those cheap sandals on a winter holiday, you stupid child of the city? Take them off and run barefoot like you did on Kiloran sands..."

Alex paused, and looked at Kemp. She made the grimace that pulled her eyebrows together into a black line.

"It was fine for him in his good leather brogues. My feet were swamped by the waves and bitter cold. The wind was whistling round our ears, and even Lindsay gave up. We went back to the car... And that was the last time I was near Lochaline House."

"But Lindsay didn't give up altogether, did he? He went back that night?"

She nodded.

"After dinner. Said he would play it sweetly—the reasonable family man. If necessary, the loving cousin."

"What time was this?"

"Must have been about half past eight. I refused to go with him. I'd spoil the cosy image—Fiona would hardly be my sort. I've sense enough for that..."

"Come now, what time did he get back?"

She looked away, uneasy.

"We had the drink in our room. You were right of course, Lennox, I was pretty drunk... and I went to sleep. When I woke up, he was there. It could have been any time... He made some strong black coffee. I remember Lindsay being furiously angry."

"Tell me what he said—his exact words. Think, Alex, think..."

Her forehead creased with the effort.

"I'll try, but it's hard to think back to what he said then, and what he said afterwards..."

"I want what was said then, that night. There would be a great deal of afterthought with Lindsay by the next day."

Alex took it slowly, picking her way through the words.

"Fiona had come to the door. She was startled to see him, and not pleased. But she did invite him in—well-trained by her mama, Lindsay said. 'Never forget your manners, Fiona, it's about all you've got.' That's what his Aunt Anna used to say to her. Lindsay had the gift of cruelly accurate mimicry—I could almost hear Fiona's mother... Anyway, apparently they talked, Fiona and he, but not for long. It was as you thought, he could not keep the sneer from him. He'd always despised her and he couldn't hide it ... It was when he talked about her responsibilities towards the family that she changed, went sour, he said. She went on about how she'd been cheated—cheated all her life. She used the word 'betrayed'..."

"By her husband?"

"Lindsay would like to have thought that... But he felt there was more to it. Something further back. He dismissed it as resentment over the way she'd been treated by her mother. But later..."

"Take it in sequence, Alex. You say they talked but not for long. What happened?"

"I think Lindsay said something like 'Where's your man tonight, out on the tiles?' and it seems Fiona went like stone. She said coldly that Fergus was away on business. Lindsay didn't believe her, of course. You guessed his very thought: her man was on the tiles all right—like a tomcat, probably in Rothesay with his mistress..."

"I know the tenor of his thinking—but did he actually say those words to you that night?"

"No, he didn't. That came afterwards—when he'd heard about Mrs. Ferguson."

"So Lindsay still thought Fergus was expected home? Fiona never told him her husband had gone to Glasgow?"

"I'm sure of it. Later when it all came out—that alibi of O'Connell's—I said Fiona'd be too ashamed to admit to her cousin—whom she didn't like anyway—that she'd been left alone all night."

"And the yacht breaking loose in the storm? Did Lindsay tell you about that?"

This time she was resolute in her negative shake of the head.

"No! You're wrong there, Lennox. That's how I know he was back before it happened. Lindsay would never lie to me. All that happened afterwards came as much of a shock to him as to everyone else. I'll swear to that. He told me that he grew angry with Fiona, said she was so close-mouthed when he tried to talk to her about the danger of marrying a man like O'Connell that he let himself go. Well, we both knew Lindsay's way with words—they would be less than charitable. I think the phrase was something about travelling men peddling their wares in every back street..." Alexina's mouth turned down. "It must have hurt, the way he said it."

"She threw him out? Small wonder."

"Not quite. She showed him the door politely, but icy cold, and slammed it hard behind him. And that was all. He came straight back to the hotel."

"But he asked you to say he'd never gone out?"

"He didn't want to get mixed up in any investigation. Said the flatfoot polis would only draw the wrong conclusions. He was so set on it being O'Connell—he didn't want the Fiscal being distracted by any side-wind. You know how mad he was when O'Connell was cleared, how obsessed he became that there was another explanation for Fiona's death than the official one. Back in Edinburgh he grew worse, gave up all pretence at study—that wasn't difficult for Lindsay—and began his own search."

"That word of Fiona's...betrayed? Did that set him off in another direction?"

She screwed up her eyes. "I think it did. But he wouldn't tell me. Said it was family, and therefore no concern of mine. Very haughty, Lindsay could be where his family was concerned—he'd like me to remember the gap between the Big House and the fisherfolk..." She gave a weary twitch of the shoulder.

"I've nearly finished, my dear Alex. Just tell me what he did."

"He went to McLintock's and suborned Miss Maggie Muir—not for the first time, as you well know. She got him out the whole of the Davison-Maclean family papers—but he was that cagey about them, never let me see much. There were boxes of them, and he took over a week to go through them. Old stuff, accounts, documents, photographs and the like. I could never see any sense in it ... Then he heard from somebody here in Bute about O'Connell being back and Lisa Ferguson joining him at Lochaline House, and he packed the lot back to McLintock's and booked us in here at the Glengariff. The rest you know. I couldn't stand it—I thought he'd gone round the twist. I needed somebody here that knew the case, somebody who'd prove to him that the official verdict was right, so he'd stop behaving like a lunatic and we could go back to having fun like we used to..."

"When he was going through these family papers, did you catch sight of any of the photographs?"

"Oh, he didn't hide those. There were some from their old days in Coronsay, and we had a laugh about them..."

"Any of Fiona?"

"That side of the Davison-Macleans were never near the Isles. Fiona's mother couldn't stand the crossing. When I was a child I vaguely remember a handsome man came once on his yacht—that would be Lindsay's uncle, I dare say. But no, Fiona was never there."

Kemp looked in his wallet. He still had the snapshot Mrs. McCready had given him. He put it on the table in front of Alexina. She picked it up, and her eyes widened.

"That's the very one Lindsay got all excited about!" She looked closely at it. "Because it was Rothesay, and because of the other girl. He said one was Fiona. That one in the striped jersey. But he wouldn't tell me who the other was, the one with the curls and the pink dress. He just put his finger alongside his nose—you know that way he had." Alex gulped, and paused for a moment. Then she handed the photograph back. ''They look a bit alike, those two little girls, even though the pink one is so pretty.''

Kemp put the snapshot back in his pocket.

''Just one more thing, and then you go and get some sleep. You said Lindsay had his spies in Bute. Any idea who they might be?''

''Jeannie up at Kilmeny Farm, for one. Lindsay must have used his charm there. It was she wrote and said Mrs. Ferguson had moved into Lochaline. Then there's some aged clerk in the Bank—he would use his money for that. I'm not meaning outright bribery— just that the Davison-Maclean money seems to loosen tongues . . . Lindsay said it was about payments made through the Bank over years. It's a Mr. Blakeney— there were letters came to Edinburgh from him but I wasn't allowed to see them. Family business, said Lindsay . . .''

''Thank you, Alex. I've tired you out, I'm afraid. Now, I have people to see, and things I must do. Can you brave your own room? I've no objection to you sleeping here, but . . .''

She smiled wanly.

''But we must observe the civilities, and no' frighten the horses!''

Kemp left her at her door. She's a Glasgow girl too, he thought, for all her Island birth; they've a strong instinct for survival in that City, life teaches them early that it has to go on.

TWENTY-TWO

W<small>HILE</small> L<small>ENNOX</small> K<small>EMP</small> <small>SAT</small> in his car across the square
from the Bank, waiting impatiently for the morning
opening hour, Sergeant McKelvie was also gazing at
closed doors. He'd rapped twice with the knocker at
Lochaline House but there had been no answering stir
inside. Now he struck again, peremptory this time.
Might as well get it over with. He'd like to have been
seeing Lisa Ferguson in other circumstances but he
tried to put the thought from him. It was a long while
since he'd gone up the wee stair beside her salon, glad
to be in out of the rainy street and off his beat on a
cold night.

He'd been a younger man then, aye and a more
foolish one, he reckoned. Now in a position of responsibility and with a wife to keep content, he'd no
great liking for his task this day. But it was up to him
to take her statement about the events of the previous
night, and tidy up any loose ends before the inspector
arrived. He'd had O'Connell at the station earlier
along with the farmer, Peter Gallachan, interviewed
them separately in a proper manner, and found their
stories tallied in every detail.

According to the farmer, he'd nearly reached the
gate of Lochaline House itself when O'Connell's car
came rattling down the road behind him. In Gallachan's word, "the man wis half-seas over," and bel-

ligerent, demanding to know what Gallachan wanted
at that time of the night disturbing Mrs. Ferguson.
Gallachan explained that a shot had been heard. That
sobered O'Connell and he couldn't get into the house
quickly enough. Peter Gallachan had followed him in.
The light was on in the parlour, and the housekeeper
was sitting sewing and watching the television. She'd
heard nothing. In the farmer's words: "She seemed a
respectable enough widow woman to me, and no' in
the least upset." "There's always someone out shooting over the loch," she'd said, bustling about and
getting them cups of tea, and Gallachan's impression
was that she was more concerned at her employer's
drinking than about the noise of a shot. Finding his
fears groundless, and being curious to see more of this
housekeeper—Gallachan was a newcomer to the
Island and knew Lisa Ferguson only by hearsay—he
had stayed to have some tea. He had been a witness to
the scene when the police arrived with the news that a
body had been found.

"O'Connell had been at the bottle again. When
your constable laddie said they thought it was Mr.
Davison-Maclean that was shot, the man just keeled
over. Flat on the floor he went. She took charge then,
got him upstairs to his bed wi' my help. 'He's no' fit
to answer their questions,' she said, and she was right.
O'Connell was in a drunken stupor. But she's a capable woman, that Mrs. Ferguson, whatever else they
say aboot her. She shoo'ed them all out—well, ye
know all that—said they could see Mr. O'Connell in
the morn when he wis in a better state."

Well, McKelvie had had him picked up at eight o'clock and taken to the station. The questioning, and the checking up on his answers had been unsparing. The sergeant scratched his head and looked up now at the blind windows of Lochaline House. Behind one of them O'Connell would be catching up on his sleep, or maybe abating his hangover with the hair o' the dog. For they'd had to drive him home once more, free from suspicion. Another tragic death at the loch—and Fergus O'Connell with another watertight alibi.

Frustrated, McKelvie gave the door a mighty thump.

He heard the sound of footsteps. Then she opened the door, and stepped back into the shadowed dark of the hall. But she made no move towards the parlour, nor did she invite him further.

Mindful of his authority and determined that the past should not intrude into the present business, McKelvie was somewhat relieved by her attitude. She didn't mean it to be a cosy chat. So be it. He produced his notebook.

There were two high-backed chairs on either side of a towering grandfather clock. She drew one out for him and seated herself on the other. In her workaday clothes, her hair tied up in a scarf with only a wisp of its colour showing to remind him of the woman he'd known, she looked different, more of the matron, less—far less—of the amorous miss. She's aged too, McKelvie thought, but then it's been years since I shared her rosy bed.

"I didn't hear you at the door," she said, smoothing her skirts, adjusting her apron. "Were you there long? You gave such a great knock on the door. Scared me a bit after all that's happened. I was taking up Mr. O'Connell's breakfast.''

''Well, now, Lisa, I'm no' going to bother you if I can help it. I only want a statement from you about last night, it all going on so near the house. Did ye no' hear anything?''

She answered him very composed, with just a hint of the vernacular to match his own.

''Mr. O'Connell went off about eight o'clock to meet that old friend of his—he'll have told you no doubt—that Mr. Lyons that's staying at the Royal. He'd had his supper and he said not to wait up for him as he'd be late. Well, ye'll ken that would be the way of it—they'd be drinking to closing time. I'd often said to him to watch out for his driving, but he'd pay no heed. He's a reckless one with a car at any time, but after all he's been through with the police in the past, who's to blame him?''

McKelvie nodded, acknowledging that Fergus O'Connell wasn't the kind to worry overmuch about drinking and driving. Indeed, the police had trailed his car the night before all the way out from Rothesay— they on the road to Kilmeny Farm in response to Mrs. Gallachan's call, he on his irregular course homewards. They'd watched him take the turn-off to Loch Aline, the time tied in with his meeting with Peter Gallachan. It made his alibi impregnable.

''Anyway,'' the woman went on, ''I put away the supper things and set about some sewing. I'd the television on, saw the news and then there was a film. You'll mind how I was always the one for the cinema? This had Steve McQueen—a grand film it was, with that great car chase in it, very noisy. I doubt if I'd have heard a shot at my very door through that din..."

It was exactly what she had told the constables the night before.

McKelvie closed his notebook and got to his feet.

"Well, thank you, Lisa. Had you ever seen Mr. Lindsay Davison-Maclean? He was skulking about here for the last few weeks."

"Never set eyes on him."

"It'll likely turn out that it was an accident. I'll not bother you again, I hope."

Something in her movement as she pushed back her chair gave him pause.

"Will ye be stayin' on here wi' yon O'Connell man? It's no' the right place for you, Lisa. I mind the days when..."

She almost pushed him away with her gesture, although he had taken no step towards her. No sun reached this part of the house, and her face was shadowed by the height of the clock.

"None of that, now," she admonished him sharply, and she was quick to open the door. She didn't come out with him on to the porch, but turned away, and he heard the patter of her feet on the stairs. She's away up to O'Connell, McKelvie thought ruefully, feeling like a slapped schoolboy. Ah weel, maybe I shouldna hae tried it.

THERE HAD BEEN no great rush to enter the Bank when the doors opened so Lennox Kemp got first bite at the cherry-cheeked girl at the counter.

"Mr. Blakeney? No, I'm sorry, he's no longer with us. Did you not know he retired last week?"

"No, I didn't. Well, well, after all these years . . ."

"We thought he'd become part of the fittings—and nearly as indispensable. You're English, aren't you? I can tell by the accent."

"So are you. Snap."

They beamed at each other like strangers met on a foreign shore.

"They let you work here without knowledge of the language?"

"There's an interpreter when things get sticky."

It was a cheering little exchange which left Kemp with true Treasury notes in his pocket instead of the colourful native issue that he was inclined to regard as monopoly money, a brief sketch of the retired Blakeney, his address and the directions to reach it.

At the pleasant stone house on the Ascog Road drilled ranks of marigolds edged the pebbled path, and standard roses, stiff as soldiers, guarded the windows placidly open-eyed to the waters of the Firth. The magic name of Davison-Maclean gave Kemp entry.

As trim and neatly turned out as his garden, Mr. Clive Blakeney lived alone. "I've always managed for myself," he said, leading his visitor into the sitting-room and waving him into a comfortable chair. "The hand of woman has never set foot in my domestic scene." He chuckled at his own joke, and rubbed his hands together. "Coffee?"

When it came, it was hot and slightly peppery, not unlike Mr. Blakeney himself, a small portly man, somewhat pompous but genial, a miniature Hitch-cock or a cartoon Pop.

"And how is Mr. Davison-Maclean? It's been a week or so since we corresponded."

Kemp's coffee jumped out of the cup, spotting the chair cover. His host hastily mopped it up with a convenient duster—he'd been disturbed at his household chores. Kemp realized that, having no womenfolk and being now retired, he was possibly immune to town gossip.

"I'm sorry to have to tell you that Mr. Lindsay Davison-Maclean is dead."

"Dear me." Clive Blakeney was a mild man despite his choleric appearance. Nothing exciting had ever happened to him, and even when Kemp explained the circumstances, without frills, his reaction was in keeping with his temperament.

"Dear me," he repeated, "What a very nasty thing to happen. Dangerous things, guns. I'm a fisherman myself. I never met him, you know. We have a mutual friend in Edinburgh—a Miss Muir. It was she who put him in touch with me. He wanted some information—well, of course I couldn't give it to him. It was confidential, you understand. Bank records. Tut, tut. Couldn't do that . . ."

He pursed his lips and looked grave, but his eyes were twinkling.

"So you weren't able to help him?"

"Not directly. But he was a very persistent young man. You see, Mr. Kemp, although I worked for the Bank here in Rothesay all these years, I do have a hobby of my own. I'm a bit of an amateur genealogist—very amateur, I'm afraid, but it gives me an interest. This is a small island but we do get a lot of people nowadays who want to trace their ancestors—even English folk like yourself. Lots of people come from overseas looking for their roots..." He blew out his cheeks and gurgled with inner amusement. "Sometimes these roots are deep into sheep-stealing, but no matter, no matter... That way, I study a lot of the local families."

"And was Mr. Davison-Maclean interested in a local family?"

"Not exactly. Have some more coffee. It's none of that instant stuff. I grind the best berries, and it's filtered."

Mr. Blakeney was enjoying himself, and was not to be hurried. Perhaps time was beginning to hang a little heavy on his hands after the exigencies of banking routine.

"Well, it would have been quite unethical for me to have told Mr. Davison-Maclean what he wanted to know, even though I had all the information on the records at the Bank. But his inquiry intrigued me, or rather his name did. Yes, it was his name cropping up like that... Because there was a kind of—er—cross-reference to a family I happened to be looking up at the time. Quite a coincidence that, wasn't it?"

Mr. Blakeney seemed to have a penchant for intrigue—and for spinning out a story.

"So what did you do to help him?"

"Oh, I just sent him along some details of the family I was working on, and let him draw his own conclusions. There was nothing wrong in that."

"And can you tell me now what family that was?"

"Well, I don't think that would be entirely proper."
He folded his arms closely to his chest. "I would have
to know your interest, Mr. Kemp."

Kemp sighed. This man should have been in MI5—
his talents had been wasted in the Bank. However, he
proceeded to fill him in as to his own background—or
so much of it as he deemed necessary. By the time he'd
finished, the chubby face opposite was aglow with
hidden knowledge, the eyes blinking with suppressed
excitement; at any moment he'd go off pop like a burst
bottle.

"But, my dear Mr. Kemp, you already know it all.
You don't need me to tell you. There, I haven't said a
word, have I?"

His merriment was infectious. Kemp couldn't help
smiling with him. "Indeed you haven't, Mr. Blakeney. You've just confirmed what was mere supposi-
tion on my part. These payments made over the years
through your Bank—Mr. Lindsay had found out
about them?"

Mr. Blakeney spread his hands on his podgy knees.

"That's not for me to say, but after all he's the
nephew. It could be something caught his eye in the
family papers at the Edinburgh end. What he wanted
to know from me was the name at this end—which of
course I could not give him since it was confidential."

"But you sent him somebody else's family tree ...
You're smart as well as discreet, Mr. Blakeney. I
gather you sent him this quite recently?"

"Let me see now. It would be towards the end of
June. I was going to retire in July anyway, and per-

haps that made a difference to my thinking... I felt it could do no harm after all this time. Is that what brought him to Bute?''

''I think it did.'' It also brought him to his death but these words were not for Mr. Blakeney's ears.

''I have used the name you didn't mention,'' went on Kemp cautiously. ''May I ask if you yourself know the lady we're talking about?''

Blakeney shook his head. ''I think I met the mother on one or two occasions. There was a final payment made on the death of the—er—benefactor, and I believe I met her then, but she died herself some years ago. You're asking about the daughter... No, I don't know her personally, only as one of many Bank clients. She seems to have kept her head above water despite a rough upbringing and not much education. She and her mother had a hard struggle—oh, the payments must have helped but they were never designed to take account of rises in the cost of living— more a gesture of conscience, I suppose. And of course the daughter has never known about the money. That was always implicit in our instructions.''

''Surely her mother would have told her before she died?''

''I don't think so. She'd given her word she wouldn't—in case of scandal at the other end—and anyway the mother was killed outright in a road accident, there wouldn't have been time for any deathbed revelation. It did come to my mind when he wrote to me that young Davison-Maclean might put two and two together, and might want some kind of reconciliation. No one bothers about old scandals these days.''

It wouldn't be reconciliation Lindsay would be thinking of; retribution was more in his line.

"Your confidence is safe with me," Kemp assured Mr. Blakeney as he rose to go, "that is, unless it's required by a higher authority."

"What confidence, Mr. Kemp? I've told you nothing. And I understand the person we may have spoken about has sold her little establishment and left the Island. The transaction went through the Bank—there's no secret about that. What surprised me was the competent way she handled the sale. She used to be what I would call feather-brained. Not that she wasn't honest," he hastily amended, fearing he might be casting aspersions on a customer, "just frivolous about money—empty-headed, well, you know what females are like..."

Not good businessmen, in Mr. Blakeney's eyes.

"She has returned to Bute," Kemp remarked casually when they had reached the door. "She's gone as housekeeper to Mr. O'Connell out at Lochaline House."

"That poor fellow whose wife drowned this winter? Well, well. The name had not escaped me. Mr. Davison-Maclean told me when he wrote first that Mrs. O'Connell had been his cousin—it drew his attention to our small island. Dear me, what a pair of tragedies in one family. But I've seen it happen in others—some families are magnets for disaster. Dear me, yes..."

Kemp felt like prodding him in his stout, complacent stomach.

"I've met the lady in question. She's an attractive woman. Perhaps she won't be a housekeeper for long..."

Mr. Blakeney's face crinkled in a smile.

"One of the advantages of avoiding womankind, Mr. Kemp, is that you close your mind to gossip, and so you think well of everyone. You should try it." He chuckled merrily, and Kemp gave up. He'd get nothing more out of this contented man, happily retired, with his fishing and his garden, his neat house, and his absorbing interest in other people's lives; he had never allowed female intrusion, and yet here he was unrepining, and as bouncy as a sand-flea.

Maybe there was a lesson somewhere in that.

In the meantime, Kemp was satisfied. Mr. Blakeney had been only too glad to show him his work on one of the island families. "You'll not be interested in the old sheep-stealers," he'd said, "just the more recent history. Lost at sea? Ah well, it's a big place, the sea."

TWENTY-THREE

IT WAS AFTER MIDDAY when Kemp drove through the town to the police station, edging past insensate pedestrians whose chosen territory extended beyond the pavements and into the roadways. Today they wore raincoats, cardigans and cloth caps—and apprehensive expressions as they gazed skywards. The fine spell was petering out in high thin cloud that mazed the sun, and a chilly breeze that sent ice-cream cartons skittering round the corners.

McKelvie was not long back from Lochaline House, still smarting from Lisa Ferguson's rebuff, although he blamed himself and was the more irritable on that account. He gave Kemp a perfunctory nod, and busied himself with the papers on his desk; he wanted no truck with the Englishman at that moment.

Kemp pulled up a chair, sank into it and took out his cigarettes; he meant to be here for some time.

"The inspector's arrived. He's in with the medical men," said McKelvie in a brisk, dismissive tone, but Kemp was not to be put off. He wasn't ready for Inspector Duncan yet either. He was not sure enough of his facts, or where they fitted. Before he took his tale to the Captain, as it were, he'd try it on the First Mate.

"I know you're busy, and you're harassed, but I think I can help," he began, in a voice just short of ingratiating.

The sergeant wanted to keep him firmly in his place, that of a bystander, his friendship with the dead man possibly relevant but no more.

"Ye've been checked up on, Mr. Kemp, you and Miss Angus. Neither of you were out o' the Glengariff last night till ye came to identify the body."

Kemp raised his eyebrows but kept silent.

"The night staff's reliable. Ye didna think we were daft enough not tae ask them? Ye see, it looked a rare funny situation... You come up here all the way frae England, Mr. Davison-Maclean rents that bothy, and there's his girlfriend and you together in the hotel. How does it look to you?"

Kemp laughed.

"I give you full marks, Mr. McKelvie. You thought I might have shinned down the drainpipe, driven out there and shot him? Or maybe Miss Angus did? I'm not blaming you—any competent police officer would have thought of that possibility. But you know that neither of us went out?"

McKelvie grunted. "There's mony rich folk come to that hotel in the season—they've got to have a security system... Both of you were in your rooms from half past ten onwards—and no' thegither, either... Ye didn't take the inquiry amiss, then?"

"Not at all. But I've got something far more serious to tell you..."

At the mention of Mrs. Ferguson's name, the sergeant bristled.

"I've a mind tae warn you to be careful, Mr. Kemp. We're no' talking gossip now. I've known Lisa all my life, and I'll warrant she's no' mixed up in this..."

"But she is—right up to those pencilled eyebrows of hers. Just listen, man... Was she not Elisabeth McFie when she was at school with you?''

"Aye, that's right."

"And her mother was Morag McFie, and there was no father? You told me that yourself. But I know who her father was, and I think Lindsay knew... Lisa—as you call her—is the daughter of Jock Davison-Maclean. She's a half-sister of the Fiona O'Connell who was drowned, and a cousin to Lindsay who was shot. Illegitimate, of course. Jock Davison-Maclean sent regular payments to Morag McFie to bring up his bastard daughter. If you want proof of that, it's all in the records of the Bank here in Rothesay.''

It took time to sink in. The sergeant's mind was not a quick-thinking machine—more cogs and pulleys than computer, but it worked none the less with logical simplicity, although when he spoke it had not reached the full implications of what he had just heard.

Ruminating on past history, as he had seen it, he said slowly: "Aye, I can see that could be the way o' it. Morag McFie was never a very forthcoming woman. Kept herself tae herself. And they say she was verra pretty as a young girl. Folks did wonder when she put that tale about, that she'd a husband lost at the sea. She was away for a while and then came back wi' the bairn. Ye say there's records o' payments? That'd clinch it..." He paused, and his deep blue eyes darkened. "Whit ye're trying to tell me is that Lisa knew she was mixed up wi' the Davison-Macleans...and when O'Connell came wi' his missus..." He struck the desk with a great blow from his fist. "I'll no' believe it!"

"And why not, Sergeant? O'Connell could have let slip Fiona's maiden name—he likely boasted of it, double-barrelled as it was... Then he and Lisa planned to kill Fiona and live on her money."

McKelvie sat still, with his unpleasant thoughts.

"We know O'Connell wasn't there that night. You're saying that Lisa was his accomplice... That she was the one that drowned the puir woman?" Again he struck the desk, an outlet for the strength of his feelings. His face was darkly flushed. "I do not believe it!"

Kemp watched him for a moment.

"Neither do I," he said quietly. The sergeant stared at him.

"Neither do I," Kemp repeated, "but Lindsay did. That's what brought him back to Bute. He'd found out the relationship of Lisa to his family. He thought she'd planned it to get even with them, maybe make a claim on Fiona's fortune. When the estate was all left to O'Connell she latched on to him. I think I know the tenor of Lindsay's thought—my own mind was not far from it."

Sergeant McKelvie rose heavily to his feet.

"I'll need to get Inspector Duncan in on this. I canna handle it myself any longer..."

"Sit down, man," said Kemp. "Before we go to the inspector I need more information—something only you can give me. I have to know more about the kind of person Lisa Ferguson is, and why you're so adamant she couldn't commit a murder—or maybe two."

McKelvie slumped into his chair.

"It's just no' her. She's no' like that. You said planning and all... Lisa couldna plan beyond the end o' the day unless maybe to shop for a few dresses or have her hair done... How can I explain?"

"Go on," said Kemp, "you're doing fine."

"She's no great brain, Lisa. And she's no' that fond o' money. I'm trying to think now what she'd do if she'd found out she was related to ony great Edinburgh gentry... She'd laugh, that's what Lisa'd dae—laugh. Aye, and tell everybody in Rothesay. That's Lisa..." He relapsed into silence.

Featherbrained. Empty-headed. That was what Mr. Blakeney had said. He had been surprised she had been competent to sell her business.

Something was wrong here. Kemp could feel it in his bones, and he trusted his bones.

"Let's get back to that February night, Sergeant, and look at the whole scene again, leaving out O'Connell. He seemed such an obvious suspect that your men had to concentrate on him... Did you think of Lindsay Davison-Maclean?"

The sergeant had been winded, but he was recovering; he was proud of his memory and keen to demonstrate its capacity. "Aye, we did—him being related to the dead woman. But he was in the clear. That girl o' his, she swore he'd been wi' her all that night in the hotel here. Quite a wee frequenter o' hotels, the silly lassie... Why's she no' at her buiks?" It was the sort of off-the-cuff remark a father might make, and Kemp ignored it.

"He had motive enough, he didn't know she'd made that will. In fact he must have been ready to kick himself when he realized she'd done it out of spite."

Kemp gave the sergeant the gist of Lindsay's meeting with Fiona on the Saturday night she died. "The fact that she'd time to make it at all means that she was alive when he left."

McKelvie looked dubious. "He could've gone back. Or do you believe his girlfriend?"

"Yes," said Kemp, "I believe her. He'd have told her if he'd seen the yacht adrift and Fiona go out on the jetty. I think he'd even have told her if he'd been responsible for Fiona drowning. Don't ask me how I know, just take my word for it. It was in Lindsay's nature to confide in Miss Angus—at least until lately... I'm certain that he was well away from Lochaline House when that storm blew up. But there were many hours to go before the morning... Let's take another hypothesis. Lisa Ferguson. Lindsay's theory, once he knew the truth about her parentage, was that she was in it with O'Connell, he with a safe alibi up in Glasgow—where was she?"

Reluctantly, like pulling out his own teeth, McKelvie brought out the words.

"She was seen by Lachie the butcher about seven o'clock. She had a cheery word with him, said she was clearing up her flat ready for her trip on the Sunday morn. Lachie packed up his shop about nine that night and was away hame. Her light was on then. The men at the ferry saw her on the first boat—cracked a joke wi' her... It's no' possible, Mr. Kemp, it's just no' possible she could have been out at Loch Aline."

"There's a lot of hours we haven't filled. Fiona O'Connell drowned at some time between eleven that night and ten the next morning—in fact the pathologist narrowed it down to between eleven and three, said the body had been in the water a good many hours..."

"If Lisa wis at Loch Aline, how'd she get there? She didna drive."

"She couldn't drive a car?"

"She never learnt. Said she didna need a car. And everybody in Rothesay knew Lisa... There's naebody would take her out there on a night like that, and no' remember it—not after what happened at the loch. Our investigation was thorough, Mr. Kemp. We never found a soul that was near the place. Ye see, it's all havers, this tale about Lisa being involved," he ended fiercely.

"All right. So she couldn't drive. I'll bet Lindsay didn't know that little interesting fact. And she wasn't clever, and she was no good at planning...and, from my reading of him, neither could O'Connell—at least not anything on this scale..." Kemp was talking more to himself than to the sergeant. "Lindsay found a photograph." He tossed his own print on to the desk. "He got very excited about it. You see the likeness?"

McKelvie stared at it. "That's Lisa McFie—just as she was when she was at the school. She'd the bonniest blue eyes, and golden curls." He seemed sorry to hand it back. "And the other lass?"

"Oh, that's Fiona. It was taken here in Rothesay—on Jock Davison-Maclean's yacht. It gave me the clue I needed—but you don't need to know about my part. But it set Lindsay on the trail, he made inquiries, found out about Lisa and then he hears she's come back and is settled in with O'Connell. So he puts two and two together and makes—five?"

The sergeant was plodding along behind him, but not too far behind.

"I see what you mean. He's going to try and pin his cousin's death on Lisa? With a gun?"

"To threaten her with. To get the truth out of her and O'Connell. Because we mustn't forget O'Connell, and whatever measly rôle he played in all this. You've had him in about last night's doings?"

"Ye'll no credit it, Mr. Kemp, yon man's a marvel. Got another cast-iron alibi. He wis drinking with a pal o' his at the Royal till after closing time. Didna leave till near eleven—and ye'll mind that's when Mrs. Gallachan heard the shot—and then he wis trailed a' the way frae Rothesay by our ain police car!"

Kemp rubbed at his forehead.

"And yet it's O'Connell has the key to it all. What's holding him back? What keeps him sliding from under us every time? Lindsay's hate, then Lindsay's vengeance...how'd he manage to escape it?"

"Well, he's got the money and a' the estate. Ye'd think he'd be happy, but he's certainly no' that. The man's a wreck..."

There was a loud knock on the door of the sergeant's room, interrupting them. Inspector Duncan strode in.

"I think you can close your file on this one, Sergeant. An accident, I'm afraid. There'll be the usual formalities, of course, but our medical friends seem satisfied. He'd had a bit too much to drink, Mr. Davison-Maclean. Stupid thing to do, climbing a wall on a dark night with the safety-catch off. Lost his footing and—wham..." He caught sight of Lennox Kemp and stopped, staring.

"You do turn up at the oddest times. Like Banquo's ghost, eh?"

McKelvie was struggling to his feet. He retained his calm, and spoke with slow resolution.

"I don't think it's as straightforward as it seems, sir. Mr. Kemp here as another theory..."

The inspector was quick off the mark.

"The dead man was a relation of Mrs. Fiona O'Connell. Is that what brings you back to us, Mr. Kemp?"

Kemp rose and held out his hand.

"Nice to meet you again, Inspector Duncan. Yes, it's the relationship that concerns me, you might say. I have not been party to the medical proceedings, naturally—you are satisfied this was an unfortunate accident?"

The inspector smiled cautiously. He had taken Kemp's measure during their meetings in the winter.

"Well, now, you have me on a spot. If we'd no previous background to the present fatality—and of course our forensic friends have no knowledge of any—then the death of Mr. Davison-Maclean would seem to hold no mystery. They talk about affinities with the Ardlamont case—perhaps you ken about that one, eh?"

Kemp nodded, aware of what was coming.

"The fatal injuries suffered here were apparently in the same category. The shot entered the head at close range, so close that the wad from the barrel was still embedded in the wound. You're with me, Mr. Kemp?"

Again Kemp nodded, reflecting that even an academic curiosity about past murder trials had been grist to the mill for any young student aspiring to a career in criminal law.

"We were perhaps gey fortunate in this case in having early advice from yon visiting expert. We're no' simply relying on the evidence of the local general practitioner—good man though he is."

"Could have been fortunate for someone, you mean," said Kemp, holding staunchly to his own beliefs despite others' professional expertise.

"And you'd quarrel with these findings, Mr. Kemp?"

Kemp knew enough of Inspector Duncan to realize that the officer was merely trying him out. Duncan would take another close look now at the medical evidence, if necessary with another team of doctors. But there wasn't time for that. He turned to Sergeant McKelvie.

"I think in view of the conversation we have just had we should enlighten the inspector on other aspects of this case, and afterwards—" he put emphasis on the words—"but not too long afterwards we should ask him to accompany us to Lochaline House... I only hope, so far as I'm concerned, it's for the last time. I don't think I'd even want to be a fisherman on those shores!"

TWENTY-FOUR

IT WAS AN AFTERNOON which struck at any hope the holiday-makers might have cherished that the early heat-wave would last. Black clouds clawed their way upwards out of the West, and rain was forecast. The colours of the moor were drained to a desolate grey uniformity, and on the loch the waters were steely slate, jumping with flashes of white where the storm-caps were rising in little angry flurries. The waves slapped at the reed-beds, and sent nets of spray across the wall by Lochaline House, silvering the granite.

McKelvie had brought a constable with him, but at the door Kemp shook his head.

"Stay there by the gate," he said, "If I need you, I'll be in touch..." The sergeant frowned; he didn't think this a good time for flippant remarks. Kemp was aware of Inspector Duncan watching from the car, sardonic but alert. In his opinion this was scarcely official business. But Kemp knew better; all he hoped was that it might be finished now, here on this pearl-grey afternoon with the rippling light shifting out there on the loch.

Even as he raised the knocker a chill went across his shoulder-blades. The sun had slid into the bank of cloud which closed round it like a shroud.

She didn't keep him waiting long. The door opened and there she was, very much the housekeeper in check skirt and apron, a thick jumper buttoned high on her

throat. She peered at him from the shadowed doorway.

"It's Mr. Kemp, isn't it? You came to see Fergus the
other day. I'm sorry, but he's ill . . ."

"I'm sorry too," said Kemp, trying to keep his voice
easy, "but I'd like to see him just the same. It's im-
portant."

There was a moment of stalemate. Kemp tried to
look at her properly, bobbing his head from side to
side as if he was a spectator bothered by an obstruc-
tion, she countering by a strategic retreat to within the
hall so that eventually all he could glimpse was an edge
of light-coloured apron.

This is a nonsense, he thought, and walked straight
in past her. There was neither sight nor sound of
O'Connell. The parlour was spruce and tidy, its upright furniture standing stiffly to attention. It was as
if the room had seen nothing, heard nothing and
would give nothing away.

She had followed him in, uncertain it seemed as to
her rôle. Should she play the beleaguered dame of the
castle or the merely flummoxed custodian of her master's hall? Kemp contrived to help her out.

"My intrusion is unmannerly, I know." The situation appeared to demand a somewhat high-flown
manner. "But it's essential I see Mr. O'Connell."

She sidled away from the door, closing it behind her.

"I've told you. He's ill. Really ill, I mean. It
wouldn't surprise me if he'd caught pneumonia, the
police dragging him out so early this morning after all
that upset last night. It's not as if he'd been anywhere
about when that poor man shot himself . . ."

"So Mr. Lindsay shot himself, did he? That'll be news for the Fiscal. I didn't know they'd got that far with their inquiries."

Kemp sat down in the same chair he'd occupied the other day he'd been entertained by her with coffee and small-talk about the attractions of Oxford Street. Her make-up this morning was not so certain, and had either been carelessly applied or she had not had time to achieve its former perfection.

She stood on the far side of the room, next to the door which presumably led to the kitchen, since it had been from there she had brought the coffee.

"I understood from Sergeant McKelvie that the tragedy outside last night had been an unfortunate accident... That was all I meant... But I have to ask you to go, Mr. Kemp, Mr. O'Connell can't see you—he's just not fit..."

"Perhaps he ought to see a doctor?"

"That won't be necessary. I can look after him. He'll be well enough when the police leave him alone. They've done nothing but harry him since his wife died—why can't they leave him in peace?"

She stood with her hands on her hips, the very personification of outrage. Gone was the soft Doric accent, her voice was hard, and there was no sign in her of McKelvie's cheery old schoolmate. Without conscious thought of what he did, save an overwhelming urge to get it over with, Kemp got up, strode across the carpet and grasped her roughly by the arm.

She turned her face to him in alarm at the unexpected assault, and he found himself looking straight into cold green eyes. She threw him off, and made for the kitchen door. Kemp was about to follow when he heard a wailing voice from far upstairs.

He ran into the hall, and was half way up the staircase where the great window flooded the landing with light when the voice came stronger.

"Fiona! Are you there, Fiona?"

He found Fergus O'Connell in the big bedroom where the dressing-table still held her silver-backed brushes, and the double bed the impression of her body alongside the sick wreck of her husband. O'Connell raised his head, and stared.

"Where's Fiona? She said she'd bring me a drink..."

A sly drunken smile crept over his face.

"Oh, there you are, Fiona..."

Kemp turned and caught her upstretched arm. The kitchen knife clattered to the floor as he hit her. She collapsed at his feet.

He stepped over her, and walked down the stair, and out of the house.

He felt sick.

TWENTY-FIVE

LENNOX KEMP and Alexina were once more together in the sedate luxury of the Morningside flat. Months had passed since the Lochaline murders had blazed across the headlines like a comet—to drop dead as any stone when they were swallowed up in the secrecy of the slow, solemn judicial process. It wasn't only time that had passed, and they were both aware of the change.

"We'll never be rid of it," she said suddenly, and he saw that she was in a sombre frame of mind. He wanted to contradict her but he had found that contradicting Alex was no easy way out now that he had got to know her better, and had his hard realism blunted.

"We couldn't have helped her, Alex," was all he could manage to say, and that had already been said many times; it didn't make it any more than commonplace.

"You talk like a bystander," she said bitterly, "always on the sidelines. Lindsay at least tried to do something...in his own way..." She broke off to pour herself a drink, and poised with the decanter in her hand. She gestured with her elbow at his empty glass, and he held it out to her. Although her offer was almost a conciliatory one, he still could not resist his exasperated come-back:

"Lindsay's methods would have ensured Stanley and Livingstone walking right past each other on different jungle trails!"

Anyone knowing Kemp would have realized his anger. As it was, he had riled her too and she burst out with a flash of her black eyes: "That's unfair. He only had part of the story..."

"Then he should have shared it." They had been through all this before; it was beginning to sound as stale as last week's bread. It might be only a temporary spat but it cast shadows on their future together—if indeed they had one.

"Lindsay shouldn't have gone it alone." Even as Kemp spoke he knew he was goaded by remorse, "He was living in a fantasy world, just as you were with your confounded loyalty—that old Highland story..."

She turned on him like a small tiger pouncing.

"And what about you? Doing your own thing in your own way? You're supposed to be a lawyer—a professional man—but you'd rather skulk in the shadows, gnawing at the edges of other people's lives! You with your private conscience that you keep locked up in a closet!"

Kemp stared at her. What she said hurt because it was at least partly true. He couldn't have put it better himself. She hadn't acquired this devastating gift for savage appraisal from any sociology lecture. This was something else—maybe the famous second-sight he'd heard about. This child of crofters and fisherfolk had the impish talent in her genes, not a mystic hangover from the past but an ability to cast a searchlight on the future. Whatever it was, he had no answer to it.

Quickly as her temper had risen, so it ebbed.

She threw herself down beside him.

"Oh, I'm sorry, Lennox. I shouldn't behave like this. I have a black mood on me. I keep thinking of Fiona in that prison hospital. What will happen to her?"

"There'll be a fierce fight between the psychiatrists, I'm afraid. Grace McCready is doing all she can... They've got a good man, Dr. de Lesseps, on their side, and the best Counsel in Scotland—all that money can buy."

She looked at him with round eyes.

"It makes a difference, Alex, even now. All the money. It's still Fiona's, remember. She was never dead..."

"You sound bitter, Lennox. Have you no pity for her?"

"She had no pity on Lisa Ferguson. It was cold, calculated murder. Oh, perhaps that's not what she had in mind that Saturday night when she drove into Rothesay to surprise Fergus with Lisa. She'd already caught them at it once, she's admitted it. But this time she found Lisa alone..."

Dr. de Lesseps had encouraged Fiona to write down her account of what had happened, partly as therapy, partly so that he could understand her state of mind. The McCreadys had shown Kemp the report. It made terrible reading, and he had no intention of communicating its contents to Alexina, but he could not forget the cool, almost schoolgirlish prose.

"...and the doctors say I must write about how Lisa died even if it's difficult. They're all fools, of course, because that's the easiest part because it's all so logical and clear to me for that's when I knew what a clever brain I had and that's why all the pink-and-white blondie girls would have to stop laughing at me. And my mother would be so proud of me because I'd drowned my father's bastard daughter...

It began to form in my head after I'd seen Fergus and my sister together. No, that's not quite right, I didn't know then she was my sister. I thought it was me in that bed of roses with him. Because that was what I saw, my face alongside his. My goodness, but he was surprised! There was me standing at the door and there was me in the bed as well. That's how I learned her name, Lisa Ferguson, but I knew better who she really was. Elisabeth. You don't look at your own face in the mirror all these years and not know who's there. Fergus had to tell me all about her and her mother—I expect she was a loose woman too and she got my father into her bed like this Lisa person got my husband. I worked it all out in my head, that's what you do when you're clever, you work it out and don't tell anybody. Fergus said he'd send her away but I didn't believe him. He said he was going to Glasgow that Saturday night but I didn't believe that either. My mother told me not to trust any man and she was right. She was betrayed by my father, and he had betrayed me too...

I drove into Rothesay and left the car in that slummy street and went up the stair. She'd never mended that lock! Shows what a lot of men she had going up there at night, but I was going to give Fergus and that whore of a sister of mine the fright of their lives. They'd be laughing away at me in that room of hers and romping on her bed just like the other time, but they were in for a shock.

I heard the water running in the bathroom. There wasn't any sign of Fergus, maybe he really had gone to Glasgow. She was singing in her bath and I thought I'd soon put a stop to that. She had her back to me when I went in. The water was green and I could see her long white legs and her pink body and her hair tied up in a shower cap and I just put my hand on it hard and pushed her under. It was easy, for I'm strong as well as clever. Most people don't know that, but my father said I could have been a powerful tennis player and I could handle his boat. There was a lot of splashing when she struggled and the walls and floor got covered in water but she couldn't get out. I got my hands on her throat and held her under. She was so surprised! She wasn't any match for me, for all her slim waist and good looks. There wasn't much sign of good looks by now. Her face was very peculiar by the time she'd stopped thrashing about. When she was quite still I turned her over face down in the water and filled up the bath again just to make sure. I went through everything in the flat, there wasn't much, and all the time the plan kept on growing in my head . . .

She had some stuff in her desk about her cheap little business, what a mess the papers were in. I'd have to tidy them up so I took them with me. I'm good at accounts and Fergus would help me get them straight. What a lot of worthless clothes she had. I left most of them, but there was a suitcase half-packed and I finished her packing for her and tidied the place up. There were a lot of those studio photographs of her—she must have been vain as well as silly—but I took them all, for they were going to be a great help to me, especially the colour ones, so that I could get contact lenses to match. There was a brochure for that health farm hotel on top of her handbag and my lovely idea kept on growing and getting better. It's only very clever people who have ideas that work out like that.

I got her out of the bath and rolled her into some shampoo capes she had hanging in the kitchen. It took a long time but it's as well to do things properly once you start. It wasn't much different from parcelling up laundry. Eventually I got her feet in and when she was completely wrapped up I tied the bundle up with string. I took her cases and her handbag down to the car first and had a good look up and down the street but it was deserted. It's a very run-down area, that, and anyway the street lamps were out because it was well after midnight. I went back and dragged the bundle down the stairs one at a time. I was breathless, I can tell you, when I got it across the pavement and pushed it in one side of the back seat. Then I went round the other side and pulled it in. It just looked like a bit of carpet covered in plastic so I stopped worrying about anyone seeing me. I went up to the flat again with her keys and gave the bathroom a good clean up with her big bath towels and took them along, she would need them at that health hotel where she was going for her health.

The house was all dark when I got back to it, so Fergus must have gone to Glasgow after all. I went in and got my old tweed skirt and jumpers and brought out my oilskins and sailing boots and thick stockings. I got the bundle out on the drive and undid the plastic and I dressed her. The stockings took some doing. It was blowing a gale and then it started to rain. The rain poured down on her but she wouldn't feel it any more so it didn't matter. It took a long time to drag her down the jetty and push her into the water but I had all the time in the world and I felt very strong. Fiona's little yacht was adrift in the middle of the loch but I couldn't bother about that now... When I pushed her into the water I untied the dinghy and shoved it away from the jetty and a wave caught it and overturned it on her face as it bobbed about but she wouldn't know about that. Poor Fiona was dead, and I by then was very tired..."

The writing had trailed off at that point. Dr. de Lesseps had explained: "She was slowly becoming more and more Lisa by then. You see she turns it into the third person. It's as if she's an outsider for a while looking down at both of them. Even the handwriting starts to change, it's no longer the neat script of Fiona, it begins to get larger and more sprawling..."

The account had continued:

" . . . I remember when it started to be fun. I took the case into the house and put the car in the garage and cleaned up the back seat but it only looked as if the rain had got in. Then I went upstairs and took off Fiona's wet clothes and put them in the airing cupboard, and I put on Lisa's suit that she was going to wear the next day and her underclothes. They felt strange but ever so nice. All that satin and lace, how could a woman like that afford them? I suppose all those men paid for them. The things were tight for me but she'd a coat would cover them and a gaudy headscarf like her sort wear that would go over my head. I laughed when I saw myself all dressed up with the seams at bursting point, and the bright pink blouse that wouldn't button up the front. But the colour of it suited me, and I saw something else in the mirror—my cheeks were pink too and I did look pretty. When Fergus saw her, when Lisa came back, he'd take her into his bed and tell her so. I counted her money—what a lot she'd got in her handbag to go on holiday with! And I counted Fiona's too. Fiona always kept a few hundred pounds in the house against a rainy day. The rainy day had come but when she set off to walk into Rothesay to catch the first boat—Lisa had even left a timetable out, wasn't that thoughtful of her?—the rain had stopped. She went across the fields at first just to make sure she wasn't seen, her carrying the suitcase and top-heavy with the clothes on her. Nearer the town when the early morning folk were beginning to stir she went by the high road down to the pier.

It would be that big coat she was muffled up in, and the bright scarf round her face to keep the cold out, that the men on the gangway saw, and "Ye're awa' tae the City, then, Mrs. Ferguson?" was how they greeted her. "Aye, I am that," was how she answered them. Lisa had a very common voice, and she'd heard voices like that all her life, and now that Fiona was dead the voices in her head that kept telling her what to do were like Lisa's. It was exciting..."

The more Lennox Kemp remembered of the account written by Fiona, the more baffled he became. He was aware he had been silent a long time, thinking of it, when Alex broke in upon his thoughts.

"If they find she's really schizophrenic, they'll not bring her to trial, will they?"

"I'm a layman," said Kemp, "with only a layman's knowledge of what schizophrenic illness really is. And, remember, I never knew Fiona Davison-Maclean. Few people did. She'd lived a very sheltered life. Even when she and O'Connell settled in Bute hardly anyone had seen her. Jeannie perhaps, but Fiona took good care to keep clear of her once she came back as Lisa. But it was the fact that the folks on the Island hardly knew her which made it so easy for her to take the place of her half-sister. Sergeant McKelvie had never met Mrs. O'Connell, and he wasn't there when the body was taken from the loch. With Fergus in a panic over his wife who'd disappeared from the house, no one doubted the body was Fiona's—a well-nourished woman of the right age, light-haired and the face badly damaged, wearing Fiona's clothes and been in the water some hours so it would be swollen and bloated—even Fergus was deceived. Anyway he hadn't the stomach to look closely at her... The postmortem report indicated a rosy colour in the lips and cheeks but apparently this is seen in certain cases of submersion in very cold water in winter—in this case it would have masked the difference between Fiona's own pasty skin and Lisa's more healthy complexion. But of course it was O'Connell's identification the police went on—after all, Lisa Ferguson wasn't even missing..."

"One can't help feeling sorry for Fergus, that miserable little man. But he must have recognized her when she came back?"

"Of course he did. The shock must have sent him reeling. For all the beauty treatments she'd had at the health hotel, the slimming, the bleached hair, and the contact lenses she'd got the same colour as Lisa's eyes, she couldn't hide herself from her husband, but she didn't want to anyway."

"She did it all for him." Alexina's voice was sad.

"Yes, she did it for him. She loved him with all the pent-up passion of her life. She refused to talk to the psychiatrist about any of that—said it was private, just between herself and Fergus."

"Sex must have surprised her," remarked Alex drily. "But why didn't Fergus speak out when she came back? He must have known then that it had been Lisa's body that was taken from the loch."

"I think he was too scared. She had him in a cleft stick. If Fiona wasn't dead, then he couldn't have Fiona's money. If he told the police he'd still get nothing. People aren't hanged for murder any more. His wife might go to prison for life but it could be a long life... Fergus liked the money, it was as simple as that. But it's no wonder he was like a hunted soul afterwards and took to the bottle. Lochaline House must have been hell for him once he knew the truth and was stuck with it.''

"It must have been hell for both of them..."

"Oh, Fiona was beyond that kind of feeling by then. She'd become Lisa. That's the incredible thing. From the moment she'd dressed herself in Lisa's clothes she was in another world, Lisa's world. That's Dr. de Lesseps's opinion. Even her voice, her accent, the very personality. You see, Fiona herself had always been a listener, an observer of other people—she picked up accents like a chameleon picks up colour. And we mustn't forget they both had the same father. In some families there are similarities in speech—all Fiona had to do was the accent bit and that came easily to her even though she'd never actually heard Lisa speak. She even took in McKelvie—and not just that time when he called the health farm and spoke to her on the phone—she was only practising then—but even when he came to Lochaline House. I think he was puzzled by some change in her but the man was probably confused by past feelings, maybe guilt, and it never entered his head that it wasn't Lisa... The same applied to the men on the pier when she caught the Sunday boat—she'd Mrs. Ferguson's clothes on and she'd the right accent. That three-mile walk she did across the wet fields—that took some doing, but I think by that time she'd the strength of ten, her own personality fused into her sister's, but she kept all Fiona's determination and will-power. We have to re-member Fiona was a strong woman—that lumpishness in her girlhood was possibly muscular—there was certainly no softness in her."

"You don't sound convinced that she's the victim of mental illness, that she's schizoid."

Kemp sighed.

"It's for the doctors to decide—and the court."

Alex was silent for a few minutes. Then she said: "I hope they find her unfit to plead. It will be a mercy."

"I'd say amen to that. But she shot Lindsay . . ."

Alex rose abruptly. "I need another drink," she said unsteadily. "I can't bear that part. Not yet . . ."

"You will have to bear it, as I do," said Kemp. The liquor warmed his dry throat. It gave him the courage to say the words he had come once again all the way from London to speak.

"I want to marry you, Alex."

She came back to him then, the colour in her cheeks flushing red up into the roots of her hair. Her eyes were soft as she took his hand, but she shook her head.

"I'm sorry that I can't say yes, Lennox. But it wouldn't work. We both know that. And it's not be-cause of Lindsay and all that he left me . . ."

She was right, of course. It hadn't anything to do with Lindsay Davison-Maclean, who, out of some quixotic whim or in a spirit of traditional loyalty had bequeathed to Alexina Angus everything he owned. Nor had the will been a recent one; it had been made two years ago, just after he had met her again at the University. He had never told her; she was not to know until after he was dead that he had loved her and thought her worthy of his heritage. That had been Lindsay's way.

"I have my own life to lead now, Lennox dear," she was saying. "I've not been kicked out—they're letting me do this year again and take my exams at the end of it." She squeezed his hand in a firm grip. "And don't you be going on hoping for me—please. I couldn't live anywhere but in Scotland. I'd be a fish out of water... Besides, we are just not the same kind of people, you and I. It wouldn't work for us..."

Kemp knew it as well as she did. They were more than simply years apart; they were separate countries, countries that no bridges or motorways could join in any act of union. That he should have given his heart, so long inviolate, to such a one as Alexina was only a trick of fate, and he would go on living in spite of it.

He didn't ask further why it had to be so; life was unfair and must be stoically borne. Perhaps, for all its apparent bounty, life had not been fair to Fiona Davison-Maclean either. She had tried to manipulate fate; would she be equally stoical in bearing the outcome?

Letter from Fiona Davison-Maclean, extracted from the Report of Dr. Peter de Lesseps

—Prison Hospital
Glasgow

I don't know why they want me to write all this down. That doctor says it will help to clear my mind but that's nonsense. My mind is perfectly clear. They have made me quite comfortable and I have no complaints except that there is too much starch in the food. I didn't know why I had such a pasty face when I was a girl and the spots but I know now. I learned a lot at that health place and I could have had more treatment and even cosmetic surgery as they call it, but there wasn't time and I had to get back to Fergus.

. . . I suppose I've always been clever. At school the other girls were all stupid, they giggled and showed off—them with their golden hair and nice skin. They said I was lumpish and the wrong shape. That pink-and-white creature from next door called me Pudding-face. I heard her and so did my mother, and she laughed and said I'd never get a boyfriend. But I knew I was cleverer than any of them. My father . . .

I don't want to write about my father but the doctors say I must. They say if I remember I can get cured. Cured of what? There's nothing the matter with me. There can't be anything the matter with someone as clever as me. Anyway, I do remember. I haven't forgotten, because when I was a girl it happened and nobody knew about it but me and I wasn't going to forget ever, not for the whole of my life . . .

We were in the Bearsden house and they were quarrelling. They were always having rows, or long silences when the maids were about. That was silly. All the servants knew anyway because they gossiped. But they didn't add things up like I did. I was a good listener, my mother used to say, but she didn't know the half of it. I was on the landing and their bedroom door was open. My mother was crying as usual. No wonder she spent so much on make-up, she was always repairing her face. She'd only just found out, I suppose. She'd started to open his letters. *You're sending money to that woman,* she wailed. She sounded unpleasant because she was hard underneath all those tears, like an old movie I'd seen with Joan Crawford. *You're keeping her and that little bastard,* she really yelled the words out. I knew what a bastard was and it wasn't very nice. Hetty our parlourmaid had had one and she got sent away but I knew my mother wasn't talking about Hetty.

My mother and father went on shouting at each other and I went on listening because it was interesting like in that film. Then I heard my own name. *It's not fair to Fiona,* my mother said, and my father gave a kind of snort and he roared out at her which surprised me because my father was a gentleman and I knew that gentlemen don't ever raise their voices: *You don't give a fig for your daughter, Anna, and if you really want to know, my bastard Elisabeth's far prettier than Fiona.* That's what my father said. I loved my father very much. He called me "Chucks" and took me sailing sometimes and then I was happy as a bird. He said I was his mate and a good little sailor.

It does hurt a bit to remember. That Dr. de Lesseps said I must but I'm beginning to think he's cruel too like all men and you mustn't trust any of them, not even your father. I didn't ever trust Fergus so it didn't matter about marrying him. I knew he did it for the money but he didn't know how clever I was at keeping that. Why couldn't Fergus be happy? I gave him a house and a car and lovely furniture he'd never had in his life before, and he was getting old and wouldn't be getting money any other way nor a settled home in a big place like I gave him. Why wasn't he satisfied when he had me? Why did he have to spoil everything and go with her? She wasn't clever, my sister Lisa, for all her blue eyes and golden curls. She was shallow and cheap. I could see that from her horrible little flat the night I searched it after she was dead. I was glad she was dead. I only saw her twice, well, three times if I think about Father's yacht. Funny she never knew about her father. Having a mother like that, I suppose she thought it could be anyone!

When Lindsay found Fergus and me after we'd got married he talked a lot about my duty to the family. What rubbish that was! I could always see right through Lindsay, he wanted my money for himself. Him and his airs and graces, he'd never given me anything but sneers since he was in short pants. But he'll not sneer at Fergus. As soon as he took his sneering face from my door I made sure Lindsay never saw the colour of my money. I gave it all to Fergus. My, won't he be surprised! But he's given me something no one in my whole life gave me. I don't want to write about love or the other thing ... It's mine, just me and Fergus. I thought he only wanted me prettier and I would have got prettier if he'd given me the chance and not gone whoring with my sister ...

Lindsay said I should honour my father's memory or some twaddle like that. But I knew what he didn't— that my father loved another daughter and she was prettier than me. That time we'd gone sailing to Rothesay and he said he had a playmate for me and he brought her on the yacht in a fancy pink dress and she had long gold curls but she spoke rough and she didn't know one end of the boat from another. And he took a snap of us. How he dared! Of course he didn't show that photograph at home, he sent one to Auntie Grace and I suppose he kept the other with all the papers he had about those payments to the little bastard. That old fuddy-duddy McLintock knew all right. But I didn't want to think about these things because there was a kind of shadow in the corner of my eye when I did. It wasn't nice and it hurt to think about what my father had done so I pushed the shadow away, and I never said anything about what I knew, even when my father died, for it was a great weight at the back of my head.

The weight has gone now and my mind's as light as a feather and all airy inside like an empty room. The shadow's gone too, it went when I saw her head on the pillow and knew who she was and what I had to do. You don't reckon to get betrayed twice in a lifetime. You have to do something about it, and she did.

Fergus came to see me yesterday. Poor man, what has she done to him? I said to him when I came back, Fergus, I said, Fiona's money's yours now, you can live like a laird and there's no one can touch us. We're married, so that'll help your Catholic conscience. How strangely he looked at me, as if he was haunted and couldn't take it in that I'd come back. But then he's a stupid man, Fergus, for all that he's dear to me. Dearer than life.

But he went to pieces when I shot Lindsay. Why couldn't Fiona's sneaking cousin leave us alone? Coming down the hill like that in the night with a gun! Looking for trouble. Well, he found it all right. Knocked at our door, he did. "Mrs. Ferguson?" he says in that high-falutin' voice of his, like his father's... Aye, and his breath had the same smell. They were a drinking lot—that branch of the Davison-Macleans. My mother had no time for them. But I wouldn't let Lindsay in. I kept him on the step in the dark. What nonsense he talked! Said he'd found out about the great family secret, that his uncle had a bastard daughter and her name was Lisa Ferguson. And that she and Fergus had conspired to kill Fiona, he with an alibi while she did the drowning. I'd never heard such rubbish. As if my Fergus would do a thing like that—or Lisa have the brains! It made me laugh so I couldn't stop. I said to him:

"You're a fool, Lindsay. You think you're so smart—like that time you got me up the apple tree at Briardene and took the ladder away, and you thought I'd not get down because I was so fat and frightened. But I wasn't frightened, and I crawled along the branches and got down myself, so there." He was surprised! The shock was on his face and he just said; "Fiona!" and rushed away from Lochaline House like a man demented.

Of course I couldn't let him go. Not now that he knew. He'd spoiled everything. I went after him. He was stumbling over the turf-wall screeching as if I was a ghost. He fell on the other side and the gun beside him. I took off the safety-catch like my father used to show me when he was putting his gun away after a shoot, and the gun was empty. But Lindsay's gun wasn't empty. I pulled the trigger. I cleaned it with a bit of fern and put his fingers where they would have been, and went back to the house. I washed my hands carefully and changed my clothes. I hadn't missed much of the Steve McQueen film anyway. I don't want to write about Lindsay any more. I never liked him and he's not worth the paper he's written on.

They keep saying I'll get better if I tell it all, that it will straighten my mind out but they're such idiots. As if it wasn't perfectly straightforward to me. Dr. de Lesseps keeps calling me Fiona in that smooth voice of his but of course he's talking through his hat. It's much more fun being Lisa—she's the one my father loved and she's ever so pretty.

There's a woman comes in to do my hair and she said only the other day that it was lovely hair and I had the skin to go with it. And I've got some nice undies and a tailored suit with a little cerise blouse. What a mercy it is that Fiona and I take the same size in shoes! I'll wear those strappy sandals that make my ankles look neat when I'm in the court. That's if those stupid doctors let me go...

They went in through the terrace door. The house was dark, most of the servants were down at the circus, and only Nelbert's hired security guards were in sight. It was child's play for Blackheart to move past them, the work of two seconds to go through the solid lock on the terrace door. And then they were creeping through the darkened house, up the long curving stairs, Ferris fully as noiseless as the more experienced Blackheart.

They stopped on the second floor landing. "What if they have guns?" Ferris mouthed silently.

Blackheart shrugged. "Then duck."

"How reassuring," she responded. Footsteps directly above them signaled that the thieves were on the move, and so should they be.

For more romance, suspense and adventure, read Harlequin Intrigue. Two exciting titles each month, available wherever Harlequin Books are sold.

INTA-1

ATTRACTIVE, SPACE SAVING BOOK RACK

Display your most prized novels on this handsome and sturdy book rack. The hand-rubbed walnut finish will blend into your library decor with quiet elegance, providing a practical organizer for your favorite hard- or soft-covered books.

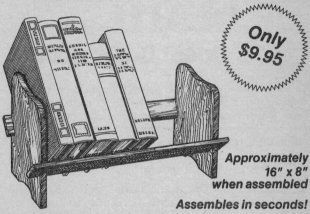

Only $9.95

*Approximately
16" x 8"
when assembled*

Assembles in seconds!

To order, rush your name, address and zip code, along with a check or money order for $10.70* ($9.95 plus 75¢ postage and handling) payable to *The Mystery Library Reader Service:*

"Miriam Borgenicht...it's doubtful that there's anyone around more accomplished at the craft."
—San Diego Union

BOOKED FOR DEATH

Miriam Borgenicht

True, Celia Summerville waited ten days before her wedding to tell her fiancé that she couldn't marry him. But she never anticipated the cold censure from their colleagues at the university—which worsened considerably when George's body turned up in a sleepy Vermont town. Dead of a broken heart—and a self-inflicted gunshot wound.

Determined to prove that cautious, pedantic George would not take his own life, Celia goes to Cedar Springs to investigate. There George, it seems, had his scholarly nose in some nasty business. A lot of people have a reason to want him dead. The question was, who pulled the trigger?

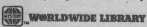